Marriage:

The Hitch and The Glitch of Wedded Bliss

By

Ivette Smith

Paperback ISBN:9781969775833

Table of Contents

Introduction

Alright, let's get real for a minute. You know that feeling when you finally sit down after a long day, ready to binge-watch your favorite show, and the remote batteries are dead? That's marriage. Welcome to "Marriage: The Hitch and the Glitch of Wedded Bliss." Yes, you'll need to bring your own batteries—a.k.a. effort, patience, and sometimes a good sense of humor.

I remember the first year of my marriage. I happily cooked, cleaned, and did laundry; we had sex regularly and held a full-time job. It was imperfect but worth the effort. He is a unique guy—yes, we are still married—but he did not have such unique ideas of what a fair marriage is. We had to go through some heated discussions that could last for days.

One memorable incident involved the dishwasher. I had just come home after a long day at work, exhausted but determined to tackle the growing pile of dishes in the sink. Just as I was about to load the dishwasher, my husband walked in and casually remarked, "Oh, don't worry about that. I like to handwash them." Handwash them? In this day and age, with a perfectly functional dishwasher sitting right there? I could feel my eye twitching. "But we have a dishwasher," I said, trying to keep my voice calm. "Yeah, but I prefer the old-fashioned way," he replied with a shrug, completely oblivious to the fact that the "old-fashioned way" meant more work for me. That night, we had one of our infamous marathon discussions. We debated the merits of handwashing versus using the dishwasher, but really, it was about so much more. It was about expectations, fairness, and the distribution of household responsibilities. It was about how we both saw our roles in this partnership. After hours of back-and-forth, a few laughs, and maybe a couple of tears, we reached a compromise. We agreed that we'd use the dishwasher more often, but he'd take charge of any handwashing that was necessary. More importantly, we agreed to communicate better and share the household chores more equitably.

That first year was a crash course in negotiation and compromise, and while it wasn't always easy, it laid the foundation for a stronger partnership. We learned that marriage isn't about who does what but about working together, supporting each other, and sometimes agreeing to use the dishwasher. So, yes, he's a stand-up guy, and we're still happily married, but it's not because we have a perfect system. It's because we learned to pick our battles and to navigate the imperfections together, one dishwasher debate at a time.

This book is here to explore how marriage isn't just a "happily ever after" fairy tale. It's a partnership that requires maintenance, like any other part of life. You can't just set it and forget it. Think of it as a living organism that needs regular check-ups, some TLC, and, occasionally, a little resuscitation.

My vision for this book is to help you transform the institution of marriage to reflect modern values of gender equality and personal freedom. We need to adapt it to our contemporary societal norms. We've come a long way from the days when marriage was basically a transaction involving a dowry and a handshake between fathers. Now, it's about love, respect, and shared goals. But transforming centuries of tradition takes some work, and that's what we'll talk about. I don't have a PhD. I'm not a therapist or a counselor. What I am, though, is a veteran of three marriages. The current being the third, and I vowed it would be the last. Because I'm Bipolar, I've had the benefit (read behind the dripping sarcasm)of multiple therapists, and I am now well-versed in looking at my marriages, past and present, with a detached, mindful attitude. Don't worry; I will not go into a litany of my successes or failures (I'd need two more books), but I am trying to give you a little perspective on where I'm coming from. I also am desperately defiant of the institution of marriage and the Patriarchy.

I firmly believe that historically, marriage has been used to control and limit women. Think about it: women were considered property, handed over from father to husband. That's a pretty grim starting point. Because so much has survived from those days, I feel there's a need to discuss marriage differently. If I had my way, people wouldn't need to get married. Fast-forward to today, and we're in a much better place, but there's still work to be done. We'll touch on some of those historical facts and examples to show why change is necessary.

In this book, we'll explore several key themes: cultural influences on marriage, redefining marriage in the 21st century, the impact of industrialization and urbanization, overcoming jealousy and insecurity, and fostering independence within relationships. We'll do this with humor and insight because, let's face it, marriage can be both absurd and enlightening at the same time.

Who is this book for? Everyone. Whether you're an adult, young adult, male, female, married, single, engaged, or in a relationship, this book has something for you. It's relevant because, at some point, we all grapple with the concepts of love and partnership, even if it's just while watching rom-coms on a Friday night.

The tone of this book will be informal, humorous, supportive, and friendly. We will keep it casual because, let's be honest, life is complicated enough without adding more formality. I want you to feel like we're having a chat over coffee—albeit a really enlightening one.

So, what can you expect to gain from this book? Practical tools and real-life examples that will help you strengthen your relationships. Whether it's figuring out how to communicate better, handle finances, or keep the romance alive, we'll cover it all. We'll focus on the absurdities of marriage—like why someone always leaves the cap off the toothpaste—and the possibilities for positive change. At its core, this book advocates for healthy, loving relationships. Exposing the absurdities of the past and offering a modern perspective encourages couples to communicate openly, support each other's dreams, and laugh together. It promotes the idea that a successful marriage is built on a foundation of trust, empathy, and shared joy. Not based on conventionalities and legal convenience. This book is both relevant and timely, offering a much-needed examination of marriage through a modern lens.

I encourage you to actively engage with the content. Reflect on your experiences and apply the insights and exercises to your relationships. Think of this book as your marriage toolkit, filled with everything you need to build and maintain a strong, loving partnership. Whether you're single, engaged, or married, this book will entertain, enlighten, and inspire you to rethink what it means to say, "I do."

So, grab your metaphorical batteries, and let's dive into the jarring, wacky world of marriage.

Chapter 1:
Foundations of Modern Marriage

Have you ever wondered why we even have marriage? I mean, it's not like we're born knowing we'll grow up, find someone, and sign a legal document to live together. The truth is, marriage has been around for ages, and not always for the reasons you might think. Before we talk about how to keep those metaphorical batteries charged, let's take a little trip back in time to see how marriage has evolved. Trust me, it's a wild ride.

1.1 Marriage Through the Ages: A Historical Perspective

Back in ancient times, marriage wasn't about love or romance. Imagine your parents meeting some other parents at a town gathering and deciding you should marry their kid. Boom, arranged marriage! In many ancient societies, marriages were arranged to secure alliances, merge properties, and keep wealth within the family. Love? That was a bonus if you were lucky. It was more about survival, politics, and economic stability. Families would often arrange marriages to strengthen ties between clans or even countries. The idea was to ensure that resources stayed within the family or alliance, and sometimes, you'd find yourself marrying a complete stranger because it was deemed beneficial.

Here are some examples of ancient laws and practices that allowed men to beat their wives and other unjust laws against women:

1. The Code of Hammurabi (Babylon, 1754 BCE):

- Marital Rights: The Code of Hammurabi, one of the oldest deciphered writings of significant length, includes laws that reflected a patriarchal society. It allowed men considerable control over their wives and permitted physical punishment.

- Law 143: If a wife was accused by her husband of neglecting her duties or causing shame, he could divorce her or enslave her in his household.

2. Roman Law:

- Patria Potestas: Under Roman Law, patria potestas (power of the father) gave a man absolute authority over his family, including his wife.

- Physical Punishment: A Roman husband had the legal right to physically discipline his wife for any transgressions. Wife-beating was considered a husband's prerogative as part of maintaining household order.

3. Greek Law:

- Lack of Legal Protection: In ancient Greece, women had very few rights and were under the control of their male relatives. There were no laws specifically protecting women from domestic abuse.

- Guardianship: Women were considered the property of their male guardians (kyrios) and had little autonomy. They could be beaten or punished at the discretion of their guardian.

4. English Common Law:

- "Rule of Thumb": A commonly cited but likely apocryphal law stated that a man could beat his wife with a stick no thicker than his thumb. While not an official law, it reflects the broader legal acceptance of domestic violence.

- Coverture: Under the doctrine of coverture, a married woman's legal rights and obligations were subsumed by those of her husband. This meant she had limited legal recourse against mistreatment.

5. The Talmud (Jewish Law):

- Husband's Authority: In certain interpretations of Jewish Law, husbands had significant control over their wives, including the right to discipline them. However, the specifics and extent of this authority varied widely among different Jewish communities and over time.

6. Islamic Law:

- Verse 4:34 of the Quran: This verse has been interpreted by some to allow husbands to discipline their wives, including the use of physical force as a last resort. However, interpretations vary widely, and many Islamic scholars argue against the permissibility of domestic violence.

7. Chinese Law:

- Confucian Principles: Traditional Confucian society emphasized the subordination of wives to their husbands. Women were expected to obey their husbands and could be punished for failing to fulfill their duties.

- Tang Code: The Tang Code (7th century CE) allowed husbands to beat their wives for disobedience or infidelity.

8. Hindu Law:

- Manusmriti: The ancient Hindu text, Manusmriti, includes verses that outline the subordination of women to their husbands and fathers. While it does not explicitly condone wife-beating, it establishes a clear hierarchy that justifies the control and punishment of women.

These examples illustrate how many ancient legal systems institutionalized the control and subjugation of women, allowing for physical punishment and other forms of mistreatment. The remnants of these attitudes have persisted in various forms across different cultures and continue to influence contemporary societal norms and legal systems. Understanding these historical injustices is crucial for recognizing the roots of gender inequality and advocating for more equitable and just treatment of women today.

Then, there was the whole business of dowries and bride prices. A dowry was essentially the bride's family giving money, property, or valuable goods to the groom's family. On the flip side, the bride price was what the groom's family paid to the bride's family. It's like a bizarre form of currency exchange, except the currency was human lives and futures. These transactions ensured that marriages were economic deals, often devoid of romantic considerations. The dowry system was particularly prevalent in societies where women had limited rights, making these transactions a way to ensure their financial security—at least in theory.

As we move along the timeline, marriage laws and customs begin to evolve. In ancient Rome, marriage was more of a social contract than a romantic union. The Romans had various forms of marriage contracts, some even allowing men to "rent" their wives. Over time, these contracts became more formalized, and the idea of marriage as a lifelong commitment started to take shape. The legal rights of women, however, remained limited for centuries. In many cultures, women were considered the property of their husbands, with little to no legal standing of their own. Marriage agreements were more about property and lineage than about partnership.

As you can see, religious doctrines also significantly shaped marriage customs. The Catholic Church, for instance, made marriage a sacrament, emphasizing its sanctity and indissolubility. This was a significant shift from earlier practices, where divorce was relatively straightforward. Religious influence ensured that marriage was seen as a divine union, not just a social contract. This shift added layers of spiritual and moral obligations to marriage's legal and economic aspects, making it a multifaceted institution.

Speaking of roles within marriage, let's talk about the traditional expectations. Historically, marriages were patriarchal, meaning the man was the head of the household, and the woman was expected to be the homemaker and child-bearer. Patriarchal structures ensured that men held power, and women were often relegated to roles that involved domestic duties and child-rearing. The concept of "separate spheres" dictated that men were the breadwinners while women managed the household. These roles were not just social norms but were often legally enforced, with laws that restricted women's rights to own property, work, or even make legal decisions.

Let's highlight some key historical shifts that brought us closer to modern marriage. The Enlightenment was a game-changer. Thinkers like John Locke and Jean-Jacques Rousseau started to promote the idea that marriage should be based on mutual consent and love. This was revolutionary, considering that marriage had been more about alliances and property. The idea that two people should actually want to be together? Mind-blowing!

The feminist movements of the 19th and 20th centuries further transformed marriage by advocating for women's rights and equality within the marriage. Activists fought for legal reforms granting women the right to own property, vote, and work. These changes laid the groundwork for more egalitarian marriages, where both partners could aspire to equal standing.

The Industrial Revolution also had a massive impact. As families moved from farms to factories, the dynamics changed. The nuclear family concept—mom, dad, and kids—became more common. Gender roles started to shift as women entered the workforce, challenging the traditional domestic roles they had long been confined to. This period marked a significant transition as couples began to share responsibilities more equally, at least to some extent.

So, here we are, standing on the shoulders of centuries of marital evolution. Marriage has come a long way, from economic transactions and alliances to partnerships based on love and mutual respect. Understanding this history helps us appreciate why marriage is how it is today and why ongoing effort is needed to modernize it.

1.2 Present-Day Marriage Dynamics:

- Rising Age at First Marriage: The age at which individuals marry has been steadily increasing, reflecting changes in societal priorities and personal aspirations.

- Pursuit of Education and Careers: More people are prioritizing higher education and career development before getting married. This trend has contributed to the rising age at first marriage, as individuals focus on personal growth and financial stability.

- Statistics: According to recent data, the average age at first marriage in many developed countries is now in the late twenties to early thirties, compared to the early twenties in previous generations.

- Cohabitation Before Marriage: Cohabitation, or living together without being married, has become increasingly common, reflecting changing attitudes towards marriage and commitment. Many couples view cohabitation as a trial run for marriage, allowing them to test compatibility and resolve any issues before making a formal commitment. The social stigma around cohabitation has diminished significantly, making it a more accepted and widespread practice.

1.3 The Shift Towards Partnership: From Control to Equality

Let's talk about how marriage evolved from a control mechanism into a partnership. Picture this: it's the early 20th century, and women are starting to demand the right to vote. The women's suffrage and liberation movements weren't just about casting a ballot; they were about asserting that women deserved a voice in every aspect of life, including marriage. These movements were pivotal in shifting the dynamics of marriage. As women gained more rights, the balance of power began to shift. Women were no longer content with being silent partners. They wanted equality, and they were ready to fight for it.

Education and employment opportunities for women also played a huge role in this transition. It was a game-changer when women started going to college and entering the workforce. Suddenly, women were not just homemakers; they were professionals, thinkers, and contributors to the household income. This shift allowed for more balanced relationships where both partners could share responsibilities. Imagine a couple in the 1950s—she's a schoolteacher, and he's an accountant. They both contribute to the household, making decisions together and sharing the financial burden. This kind of partnership was becoming more common, laying the groundwork for the egalitarian marriages we strive for today.

Legal reforms were the icing on the cake. Laws began to change, granting women equal rights within marriage. For instance, the Married Women's Property Act allowed women to own property in their own right. Divorce laws became fairer, recognizing that women had the right to leave unhappy marriages. These legal changes were crucial because they provided the framework for equality. Couples could now enter marriage as equal partners, both legally and socially. This legal foundation empowered women to stand on equal footing with their spouses, setting the stage for more balanced and respectful unions.

Modern marriages—not all, but many—are not about partnership and equality. But what does that really mean? It means shared responsibilities and decision-making. Gone are the days when the man made all the financial decisions while the woman managed the home. In a true partnership, both partners are involved in making decisions about everything from finances to parenting. Mutual respect and support are the cornerstones of this kind of relationship. Each partner values the other's contributions and supports their personal growth. Communication is indispensable here. Open, honest dialogue ensures that both partners feel heard and valued. It's about working together, not against each other.

Of course, striving for marriage equality comes with its own set of challenges and benefits. Balancing power and negotiating roles can be tricky. It's not always easy to decide who does what, especially if both partners have demanding careers. However, the benefits far outweigh the challenges. When both partners share the workload, it reduces stress and increases satisfaction. Common conflicts in egalitarian marriages often revolve around these negotiations, but effective communication can usually resolve them. For example, a couple might argue about who should handle the grocery shopping. The solution? A weekly schedule where they take turns, ensuring fairness and reducing tension.

Real-life examples of successful partnerships abound. Think about the Obamas. Both Barack and Michelle have spoken about supporting each other's careers and sharing responsibilities at home. This kind of partnership is inspiring because it shows that marriage equality is not just an ideal but a reality that can be achieved. Couples who strive for this kind of partnership often find that their relationships are more fulfilling and resilient.

Societal and cultural expectations also play a significant role in shaping modern marriages. Media portrayals of gender roles can either support or undermine efforts toward equality. For instance, TV shows and movies that depict strong, independent women and supportive, involved men can reinforce positive norms. On the other hand, traditional portrayals can perpetuate outdated stereotypes. Family and community expectations can also impact the dynamics of egalitarian marriages. In some cultures, the extended family's opinions hold significant weight, and couples may struggle to navigate these pressures while maintaining their commitment to equality.

1.4 The Role of Love and Mutual Respect in Modern Marriages

Let's talk about love, the stuff that makes the world go 'round—or at least keeps the marriage boat afloat. You see, the idea that marriage should be based on romantic love is relatively new in the grand scheme of things. Historically, marriages were more about alliances, property, and social status. But somewhere along the way, people started to think, "Hey, wouldn't it be nice if we liked the person we're going to spend our lives with?" Enter the 19th and 20th centuries, when the "love match" concept began to take center stage. Literature and the media made romantic love the gold standard for marriage. Writers like Jane Austen and poets like Lord Byron romanticized the idea of marrying for love, making it seem almost rebellious and undoubtedly desirable. Movies, novels, and even music have continued to push this narrative, making us all believe that love should be the cornerstone of any marriage.

Mutual respect, however, is the unsung hero of a lasting relationship. Think of it as the glue that holds everything together when the honeymoon phase is a distant memory. Mutual respect means understanding and valuing each other's perspectives, even when you don't agree. It's about recognizing that your partner is an individual with their own thoughts, feelings, and boundaries. Respecting those boundaries and encouraging each other's growth is crucial. Imagine your partner wants to take up a new hobby, like painting. Even if you have zero interest in art, supporting their passion shows respect for their individuality. These small acts build a foundation of mutual respect, making the relationship prosperous and more resilient.

So, how do you foster love and respect in your marriage? Start with daily acts of appreciation and kindness. It doesn't have to be grand gestures; sometimes, a simple "thank you" or "I appreciate you" can go a long way. Effective communication techniques are also vital. Make it a habit to engage in active listening, where you truly hear what your partner is saying without planning your rebuttal. This simple act can make a world of difference in how loved and respected your partner feels. When conflicts arise, and they will use conflict resolution strategies that prioritize respect. This means addressing the issue at hand without resorting to name-calling or bringing up past grievances. Focus on finding a solution that works for both of you rather than trying to "win" the argument.

Of course, maintaining love and respect isn't always a walk in the park. Stress and external pressures can take a toll on any relationship. Whether it's work stress, financial issues, or family drama, these external factors can strain the bond you share. It's important to recognize these stressors and address them together as a team. Dealing with differences and disagreements is another common challenge. No two people are exactly alike, and differences are bound to arise. The key is approaching these disagreements with an open mind and a willingness to understand your partner's perspective. Self-care and personal development also play a crucial role. When you take care of yourself, you're better equipped to be a supportive and loving partner. This means making time for activities that rejuvenate you, whether exercising, reading, or spending time with friends. I read somewhere that "the number one decision that will determine 90% of your happiness or misery is marrying the right person." Think about that.

In modern marriages, love and mutual respect are not just ideals but necessities. They are the bedrock upon which a healthy and lasting relationship is built. While the notion of romantic love has evolved, the need for mutual respect has remained constant. By fostering these qualities, you can navigate the ups and downs of marriage with grace and resilience. Remember, it's the little things—those daily acts of kindness, effective communication, and unwavering support—that make all the difference. So, keep those batteries charged, and your marriage will continue to thrive.

1.5 Cultural Influences on Marriage: East Meets West

Imagine the scene: a grand wedding in India with vibrant colors, intricate rituals, and hundreds of guests. Contrast this with a small, intimate wedding in the U.S., where the couple writes their vows and maybe even includes their dog in the ceremony. These snapshots highlight the vast differences in Eastern and Western marriage traditions. In many Eastern cultures, arranged marriages are still common. Families play a significant role in choosing the spouse, ensuring that the union benefits the family economically and socially. Meanwhile, love marriages dominate the Western landscape, where the couple's romantic connection is the primary driver for tying the knot.

Family and community often have a decisive say in Eastern marriages. Parents, elders, and sometimes even the extended family weigh in on the decision, ensuring it aligns with cultural and social norms. In contrast, Western marriages tend to prioritize individual choice, with the couple making decisions independently. This difference can lead to unique challenges, especially in cross-cultural marriages, where one partner might expect family involvement while the other values autonomy. Navigating these expectations requires open communication and a willingness to compromise.

Cultural rituals and ceremonies also differ widely. Eastern weddings might include multiple days of celebrations, intricate customs, and elaborate attire. For instance, an Indian wedding might feature a Mehendi ceremony, where intricate henna designs are applied to the bride's hands, followed by a Sangeet, a musical night filled with songs and dances. Western weddings, on the other hand, often focus on the ceremony and reception, with traditions like the exchange of rings, the first dance, and cutting the wedding cake. Each set of traditions brings its unique charm, but blending them in multicultural societies can be both exciting and challenging.

Globalization has blurred some of these lines. As people move across borders and cultures mix, marriage traditions evolve. Cross-cultural marriages are becoming more common, bringing together different customs and expectations. These marriages require a delicate balance of respecting each other's traditions while creating new ones that reflect the couple's unique blend. For example, a couple might decide to incorporate both a traditional Indian ceremony and a Western-style reception, blending the best of both worlds. This blending of traditions can enrich the marriage, providing a deep sense of cultural connection and mutual respect.

The concept of cultural adaptation is crucial for couples from different backgrounds. Negotiating cultural expectations and values can be a delicate dance. It involves understanding and respecting each other's heritage while finding common ground. Developing a shared cultural identity within the marriage helps in navigating these differences. This might mean celebrating multiple holidays, adopting different family customs, or even learning each other's languages. The goal is to create a marriage that honors both partners' backgrounds while forging a new path together.

Cultural heritage continues to shape marriage dynamics today. Communication styles, for example, can be heavily influenced by cultural background. In some cultures, direct communication is valued, while indirect communication is the norm in others. Understanding these differences can prevent misunderstandings and foster better communication. Cultural sensitivity and understanding are essential. It means being aware of and respecting each other's cultural norms, whether it's how decisions are made, how conflicts are resolved, or how affection is expressed.

In summary, the intersection of Eastern and Western marriage traditions offers a rich tapestry of rituals, values, and expectations. While the differences can be stark, blending these traditions in today's globalized world creates opportunities for deeper connection and mutual respect. Navigating these waters requires open communication, cultural sensitivity, and a willingness to adapt. But in embracing these differences, couples can create a marriage that is uniquely theirs, enriched by the best of both worlds.

1.6 The Impact of Industrialization and Urbanization on Marriage Dynamics

Industrialization. The word alone makes you think of factories, steam engines, and a whole lot of smoke. But beyond the machinery, industrialization reshaped family structures in ways we're still feeling today. Picture it: families moving from sprawling farms to cramped city apartments. This shift from agrarian to industrial societies didn't just change where people lived; it altered how they lived. Extended families, once the norm, began to fragment. Grandma and Grandpa were no longer just down the hall; they were miles away in the old family home, leaving the nuclear family—mom, dad, and the kids—as the new standard. This change forced couples to rely more on each other, for better or worse.

Gender roles morphed, too. In agrarian societies, men and women often worked side by side in the fields. However, as families moved to cities, men took factory jobs while women were expected to manage the home. This division of labor reinforced the idea that men were breadwinners and women were homemakers. Fast-forward to today, and we're still grappling with these entrenched roles, even as more women enter the workforce. The dual-income household has become more common, but balancing career and home life remains a challenge. Economic necessity often drives both partners to work, but this can create stress as they juggle their careers, household responsibilities, and possibly raising kids.

Urbanization brought its own set of complications. Living in a bustling city offers countless opportunities but also numerous challenges. Work-life balance becomes a tightrope act when you're navigating long commutes, demanding jobs, and the constant buzz of city life. Social networks in urban environments can be both a blessing and a curse. On one hand, you have access to a broader support system of friends and colleagues. On the other, the fast-paced nature of city living can make deep, meaningful connections harder to maintain. The anonymity of city life means you might not have the same close-knit community that rural settings offer, making it easier for couples to drift apart if they're not careful.

Economic factors play a significant role in shaping modern marriages. Financial stability is a cornerstone of a healthy relationship, but economic pressures can strain even the strongest bonds. Dual-income households often face the dilemma of balancing career ambitions with family needs. Financial stress can exacerbate existing tensions and lead to frequent arguments. Imagine a couple where one partner loses their job, and suddenly, the financial burden falls entirely on the other. This scenario can lead to resentment and anxiety, making it crucial for couples to adopt strategies for managing money matters as a team. Budgeting, financial planning, and open discussions about spending habits can alleviate some of this stress.

Technology has revolutionized the way couples interact and manage their households. Digital communication tools like texting and video calls make it easier to stay connected, even when you're miles apart. But there's a downside. Over-reliance on digital communication can lead to misunderstandings and a lack of face-to-face interaction, which is vital for emotional intimacy. Household management has also been transformed by technology. Apps for budgeting, meal planning, and even chore tracking can streamline daily tasks, but they can't replace the need for genuine communication and cooperation.

In the grand scheme of things, industrialization, and urbanization have brought both challenges and opportunities to marital dynamics. While these shifts have changed the way we live and interact, they've also highlighted the importance of adapting to new circumstances. Couples today have more tools and resources at their disposal than ever before, but they also face unprecedented pressures. Understanding these dynamics can help couples navigate their relationships more effectively, ensuring their partnerships remain strong and resilient in the face of modern challenges.

In wrapping up this exploration of marriage's evolution, it's clear that understanding where we've come from helps illuminate the path forward. By recognizing the influences of industrialization, urbanization, and economic shifts, couples can better navigate their relationships today. Whether you're in a bustling city, balancing dual careers, or figuring out how to integrate technology into your home life, the key lies in adaptability, communication, and mutual support. So keep those batteries charged, stay connected, and remember: marriage, like life, is a journey, not a destination.

1.7 Contemporary Critiques

- Economic Dependence: Despite legal advancements, many women still face financial dependence within marriage, which can make it challenging to leave unhealthy or abusive relationships.

- Double Standards: Societal expectations around marriage often place more pressure on women regarding appearance, behavior, and responsibilities, while men may face fewer constraints.

- Labor Division: Even in modern marriages, women often bear a disproportionate burden of household chores and child-rearing responsibilities, limiting their personal and professional growth.

Chapter 2:
Communication: The Heartbeat of a Healthy Marriage

Have you ever had one of those days when you and your partner are talking, but it feels like you're on entirely different planets? You're trying to discuss dinner plans, and suddenly, you're knee-deep in a debate about who forgot to take out the trash. It's like playing a game of telephone, where the message gets garbled along the way. Welcome to the insane world of communication in marriage, where what you say and what your partner hears can be two very different things.

Imagine this: You're at a party, your partner is across the room, and you're trying to catch their eye to let them know it's time to leave. You wave, they wave back, you point at your watch, and they give you a thumbs-up, thinking you're reminding them of the time. This little dance could have been avoided with a quick, "Hey, it's getting late; should we head out?" But why is communication so tricky sometimes? The answer lies in understanding how we listen—or fail to, which brings us to the concept of active listening.

2.1 Active Listening: Turning Hearing into Understanding

Active listening is like the difference between hearing your favorite song in the background while doing chores and sitting down to listen to it with headphones, catching every beat and lyric. It's about fully engaging with what your partner is saying, not just letting their words wash over you like background noise. Active listening isn't just nodding along while planning your grocery list. It's about genuinely connecting with the speaker and making them feel heard and understood. This type of listening is essential for effective communication at large, not just in marriage, because it ensures that both parties are on the same page, fostering a deeper connection and understanding.

So, what's the big difference between hearing and actively engaging? Hearing is passive; it's what happens when sound waves hit your eardrums. You hear the car honking outside, the dog barking, or your partner mumbling about dinner. Active engagement, on the other hand, is an intentional act. It's focusing your attention on your partner, making eye contact, and responding in a way that shows you're genuinely interested in what they're saying. When you actively engage, you're not just hearing words; you're understanding the emotions and intentions behind them.

Attention and presence are the cornerstones of active listening. Imagine you're in the middle of a heartfelt conversation, and your partner is scrolling through their phone. How does that make you feel? Probably ignored and undervalued. Being present means setting aside distractions and giving your partner your undivided attention. It's about mindfulness, being in the moment, showing through your actions that what they're saying matters to you.

Now, how can you become a better listener? Start with paraphrasing and summarizing your partner's words. This doesn't mean being a parrot but echoing back what they've said to show you've understood. For example, if your partner says, "I had a tough day at work," you might respond, "It sounds like work was really stressful today. Do you want to talk about it?" This strongly suggests that you're not just hearing the words but understanding the underlying emotions.

Open-ended questions are another powerful tool. Instead of asking questions that can be answered with a simple yes or no, ask questions that encourage deeper conversation. For instance, instead of asking, "Did you have a good day?" you could ask, "What was the most challenging part of your day?" This invites your partner to share more and opens the door to a more meaningful dialogue.

Interruptions and distractions are the arch-enemies of active listening. Nothing kills a conversation faster than cutting someone off mid-sentence or glancing at your phone while they're talking. Make a conscious effort to avoid interrupting and minimize distractions. This might mean putting your phone on silent or choosing a quiet space to talk. Show your partner that their words are worth your full attention.

Of course, active listening isn't without its challenges. Preconceived notions and judgments can be significant barriers. If you go into a conversation with your mind already made up, you're not listening. Try to approach each conversation with an open mind, setting aside preconceived ideas. Emotional triggers and reactions can also get in the way. If something your partner says hits a nerve, take a moment to breathe and compose yourself before responding. Reacting emotionally can lead to misunderstandings and conflict.

External distractions like phones, TV, or even noisy environments can also hinder active listening. Creating a conducive environment for conversation can make a big difference. Choose a quiet, comfortable space where you can focus on each other without interruptions.

To practice active listening, try some exercises designed to enhance your skills. Reflective listening exercises are a great start. Sit down with your partner and take turns speaking about a specific topic while the other person listens and then paraphrases what was said. This helps both partners practice articulating their thoughts and understanding each other. Another exercise is the "listening without interruption" practice.

Set a timer for a few minutes and let your partner speak without interrupting. Focus entirely on their words and emotions. After the timer goes off, switch roles. This exercise can help you develop the habit of truly listening and resisting the urge to interrupt.

Active listening is about turning hearing into understanding. It's about being fully present, engaging with your partner, and showing them that their words matter. By practicing active listening, you can strengthen your communication skills, deepen your connection, and navigate the complexities of marriage with greater ease. So next time you find yourself in a conversation with your partner, put on those metaphorical headphones and really tune in. It's the best way to keep your relationship in harmony.

2.2 Effective Use of "I" Statements: Reducing Defensive Reactions

Picture this: You're in the middle of a heated argument with your partner. Voices are raised, and suddenly, someone says, "You always do this!" Boom. Defensive walls go up, and any chance of a productive conversation flies out the window. But what if there was a way to express your feelings without triggering those defenses? Enter the magical world of "I" statements. These handy phrases shift the focus from blaming your partner to sharing your personal experience, making it easier for both of you to understand each other without getting defensive.

So, what are "I" statements, and why do they work so well? An "I" statement is a way of communicating that focuses on your feelings and experiences rather than accusing or blaming the other person. By saying, "I feel frustrated when the dishes aren't done because it makes me feel overwhelmed," you're sharing your feelings and the reason behind them rather than making your partner feel attacked. This approach reduces defensive reactions and promotes understanding. Instead of your partner thinking, "Great, here we go again with the blame game," they're more likely to think, "Okay, I see why this is bothering you."

Let's break down the formula for creating effective "I" statements. It's pretty simple: "I feel [emotion] when [situation] because [reason]." This structure helps you clearly express your feelings and the context behind them. For example, you might say, "I feel hurt when you interrupt me because it makes me feel unheard." Notice how this statement focuses on your feelings and the impact of the situation rather than pointing fingers. It's all about making your partner understand your perspective without making them feel blamed or criticized.

But like any good tool, "I" statements can be misused if you're not careful. One common mistake is turning an "I" statement into a hidden "you" statement. For instance, saying, "I feel like you're wrong," is just a sneaky way of blaming your partner while pretending to be diplomatic. It's essential to keep the focus on your feelings and experiences. Another pitfall is being too vague. I feel bad when things aren't right" doesn't give your partner much to work with. Be specific and clear about the situation and the reasons behind your feelings to avoid confusion.

To get the hang of using "I" statements, it's helpful to practice. One exercise is the "daily reflection" exercise, where you take a few minutes each day to reflect on a situation that bothered you and practice framing it as an "I" statement. For example, if you felt ignored during dinner, you might write down, "I felt lonely when you were on your phone during dinner because I wanted to connect with you." This exercise helps you get comfortable with the structure and makes it easier to use in real-time conversations.

Another useful practice is role-playing conflict scenarios with your partner. Choose a common issue that tends to spark arguments, and take turns expressing your feelings using "I" statements. For instance, if you often argue about chores, you might say, "I feel stressed when the laundry isn't done because it adds to my workload." Your partner can then respond with their own "I" statement, such as, "I feel overwhelmed when I'm expected to do all the laundry because I have a lot on my plate too." This role-playing helps both of you practice expressing your feelings constructively and can lead to more productive discussions.

Sometimes, incorporating a visual or interactive element can make these exercises more engaging. Consider creating a checklist of everyday situations where you can practice using "I" statements.

Checklist: Practicing "I" Statements

1. During a disagreement about chores

2. When feeling ignored or unheard

3. When discussing financial concerns

4. When feeling overwhelmed or stressed

5. During a conversation about future plans

Use this checklist to identify moments when you can practice your "I" statements. Reflect on each situation and write down your feelings using the formula. This exercise helps you improve your use of "I" statements and encourages you to think more deeply about your emotions and the reasons behind them.

Using "I" statements is a powerful tool for reducing defensive reactions and promoting understanding in your marriage. By focusing on your own feelings and experiences, you can express your concerns without making your partner feel attacked. Practice daily reflections and role-playing scenarios to master this skill, and use the checklist to help identify moments when "I" statements can be particularly helpful. With a bit of practice, you'll find that your conversations become more constructive, and your connection with your partner grows stronger.

2.3 Non-Verbal Communication: Reading Between the Lines

Have you ever had a conversation with someone and felt like they were saying one thing, but their body language was screaming something entirely different? Welcome to the fascinating world of nonverbal communication. It's that silent language we all speak, often without even realizing it. Nonverbal communication includes body language, facial expressions, gestures, tone of voice, and eye contact. These elements can complement or totally contradict what you're saying, leaving your partner scratching their head and wondering what you mean.

Body language is a significant part of non-verbal communication. Imagine telling your partner you're happy for them, but your arms are crossed, and you're not making eye contact. Your body is sending mixed signals that can confuse your partner. Facial expressions are another biggie. A smile, a frown, or a raised eyebrow can all convey a range of emotions without a single word. Gestures, like hand movements or nodding, also play a role. They can emphasize what you're saying or, if misused, distract and confuse.

The tone of voice and eye contact is equally crucial. The tone of your voice can change the meaning of a sentence entirely. For instance, saying "I'm fine" in a flat, monotone voice versus a cheerful, upbeat one sends two very different messages. Eye contact, meanwhile, shows that you're engaged and interested. Avoiding eye contact can make you seem disinterested or even deceptive. These non-verbal cues are powerful tools in communication, often speaking louder than words.

Nonverbal cues can either complement or contradict your verbal messages. When your words and actions are congruent, they reinforce what you're saying, making your message clear and trustworthy. For example, telling your partner, "I love you," while maintaining eye contact and a warm tone of voice makes the message heartfelt. On the other hand, if your non-verbal cues contradict your words, it can lead to confusion and mistrust. Saying "I'm not upset" with a clenched jaw and crossed arms sends mixed signals, making your partner question your honesty.

Recognizing and interpreting non-verbal cues accurately is a skill that can enhance your communication. Pay attention to your partner's body language and facial expressions. Are they leaning in, showing interest, or fidgeting, indicating discomfort? Understanding these cues can help you respond more empathetically and effectively. For example, if your partner looks stressed, you might offer a comforting touch or a reassuring smile to show support.

However, non-verbal communication isn't foolproof. Misinterpretations can quickly arise. You might interpret a neutral facial expression as disinterest when your partner is just deep in thought. Cultural differences can also play a role. In some cultures, maintaining eye contact is a sign of respect; in others, it might be seen as aggressive. Being aware of these differences can prevent misunderstandings and foster better communication.

Strengthening your nonverbal communication skills involves mindful observation and practice. Start by becoming more aware of your own nonverbal cues. Notice how you use body language, facial expressions, and tone of voice in different situations. Practicing mindful observation can help you become more attuned to these cues. For example, focus on your partner's nonverbal signals during a conversation. Are they nodding in agreement? Are their facial expressions matching their words? This awareness can help you respond more appropriately.

Another effective strategy is using positive body language to reinforce verbal messages. Open body language, such as uncrossed arms and relaxed posture, can make your partner feel more comfortable and engaged. A genuine smile can convey warmth and approachability. Maintaining eye contact shows that you're interested and paying attention. These small actions can significantly impact how your partner perceives your message.

To make these improvements stick, try incorporating exercises into your daily routine. Mindful observation can be as simple as taking a few minutes each day to notice your partner's nonverbal cues during a conversation. Reflect on how their body language, facial expressions, and tone of voice align with their words. This exercise can help you become more attuned to nonverbal signals and respond more effectively.

Focusing on nonverbal communication can enhance your understanding and connection with your partner. Paying attention to body language, facial expressions, gestures, tone of voice, and eye contact can help you interpret and respond more accurately to your partner's messages. Being mindful of these cues and practicing positive body language can create a more supportive and empathetic communication environment. So, the next time you're in a conversation, remember to read between the lines and let your actions speak as loudly as your words.

2.4 Digital Communication: Navigating Conversations in the Digital Age

Remember the days when the only way to communicate was through face-to-face chats, handwritten letters, or maybe a phone call on a landline? Ah, simpler times. Today, we've got a dozen digital options at our fingertips—texts, emails, social media, video calls. While these tools have made it easier than ever to stay connected, they've also introduced new challenges to our relationships.

Digital communication has changed the way couples interact. On the plus side, it's incredibly convenient. You can send a quick text to say, "I love you," or share a funny meme that made you think of your partner. Social media lets you keep up with each other's lives and instantly share moments. But there are downsides, too. Miscommunications can occur more quickly in the digital realm. A hastily typed text or an ambiguous emoji can lead to misunderstandings. Plus, the constant availability of digital communication can blur the boundaries between personal and shared spaces, making it harder to disconnect and enjoy quality time together.

Social media plays a significant role in relationship dynamics. It's a double-edged sword. On the one hand, it allows couples to share their lives with friends and family, creating a sense of community. On the other hand, it can introduce jealousy and insecurity. Seeing your partner interact with others online or comparing your relationship to the seemingly perfect lives of others can create tension. It's essential to navigate these waters carefully, ensuring social media enhances rather than detracts from your relationship.

Setting boundaries for digital device usage is vital to ensuring healthy and clear communication in digital formats. Decide together when it's okay to use phones and when it's time to put them away. For instance, you might agree to keep phones off the dinner table or set specific times for checking social media. Ensuring tone and intent are clear in texts and emails is also crucial. Written messages can be easily misinterpreted without the benefit of facial expressions or tone of voice. Take an extra moment to read over your message before sending it. If it's a sensitive topic, consider having the conversation in person or over a video call to avoid misunderstandings.

Maintaining a balance between digital and face-to-face interactions is crucial. While digital communication is convenient, it can't replace the depth and nuance of in-person conversations. Face-to-face interactions allow for more emotional connection and understanding. The limitations of digital communication in conveying emotions are significant. A heartfelt message can lose its impact when reduced to a few words on a screen. Strategies for prioritizing face-to-face conversations include setting aside regular time for in-person dates or conversations. Even in long-distance relationships, video calls can provide a closer connection than texts or emails alone.

One practical exercise for improving digital communication is the "digital detox" weekend. Choose a weekend where you both agree to disconnect from digital devices. Spend this time focusing on each other, engaging in activities you both enjoy, and having meaningful conversations. This break from digital distractions can help you reconnect and strengthen your bond. Another helpful practice is "text message check-ins." Throughout the day, send brief, positive messages to each other. It could be a simple "thinking of you" or a brief update on your day. These small gestures help maintain a sense of connection, even when you're apart.

By examining the impact of digital communication on relationships, we can better navigate the benefits and challenges it presents. Setting boundaries, ensuring clarity in digital messages, and prioritizing face-to-face interactions are vital to maintaining a healthy balance. Practical exercises like digital detox weekends and text message check-ins can help couples navigate the digital age more effectively. As we continue to explore the complexities of communication in marriage, remember that the goal is to stay connected and supportive, whether you're face-to-face or screen-to-screen.

Next, we'll discuss conflict resolution and emotional intelligence, which are essential skills for navigating the ups and downs of any relationship. Stay tuned!

Chapter 3:
Conflict Resolution and Emotional Intelligence

You know that moment when you're arguing with your partner and realize things are spiraling out of control faster than you can say, "Hey, let's take a breather"? That's"where this chapter comes in. Conflict is inevitable, but how you handle it can make or break a relationship. This chapter is about giving you the tools to navigate those stormy seas without sinking the ship. And trust me, it's easier than you think—with a bit of practice and a lot of patience.

3.1 Time-Out Protocols: Preventing Escalation

Let's start with the concept of time-outs. No, I'm not talking about the kind you give a toddler who won't stop drawing on the walls. Time-outs in relationships are a way to hit the pause button when things get too heated. Imagine you're in the middle of a fiery argument, and it feels like every word is a matchstick ready to ignite. Taking a time-out is about removing yourself from the situation to cool down before things get worse. This simple act can prevent verbal and emotional abuse, giving both of you a chance to regain your composure and think more clearly.

So, how do you implement an effective time-out without turning it into an avoidance tactic? First, you need a mutually agreed-upon signal to take a time-out. It could be a word, a hand gesture, or even just saying, "Hey, I need a break." The key is that both partners understand and respect this signal. Next, set a specific time limit for the break. This isn't an indefinite escape; it's a temporary pause. Maybe it's 15 minutes, or maybe it's an hour. The important thing is that you both know when you'll come back together to talk. Finally, agree on a post-time-out discussion plan. Decide in advance how you'll approach the conversation once you return. This could involve taking turns to speak, using "I" statements, or any other strategy that works for you.

If you're not careful, common pitfalls can undermine time-outs' effectiveness of time-outs. One of the biggest mistakes is using time-outs as an avoidance tactic. It's tempting to call for a time-out and never come back to address the issue, but that only leaves problems unresolved and festering. Another mistake is failing to follow through with the post-time-out discussion. If you don't return to the table, the time-out becomes pointless. Avoid these pitfalls by committing to the agreed-upon plan and holding each other accountable.

To help you practice time-out protocols, try some role-playing scenarios where time-outs might be needed. For example, imagine you're not arguing about finances, and things start getting heated. Practice calling for a time-out, taking a break, and then coming back to discuss the issue calmly. Another helpful exercise is practicing calming techniques during the time-out period. This could be deep breathing, meditation, or even going for a walk. The goal is to use the time-out to truly calm down and collect your thoughts.

Exercise: Practicing Time-Out Protocols

6. Role-Playing Scenarios: Act out common arguments where time-outs might be needed. Practice calling for a time-out, taking a break, and returning to discuss the issue calmly. I know the idea of "practicing" for an argument sounds like a plan for discord, but we must remember that sometimes the rules of engagement must be reviewed.

7. Calming Techniques: During the time-out, practice techniques like deep breathing, meditation, or going for a walk to calm down and collect your thoughts.

By effectively using time-outs, you can prevent arguments from escalating and create a space for constructive conversation. It's about recognizing when things are getting out of hand and stepping back before saying or doing something you'll regret. Time-outs aren't about avoiding the issue; they're about creating the best possible environment to resolve it. So, the next time you feel your blood boiling, remember that a time-out might be just what you need to cool things down and come back stronger together.

3.2 Structured Conflict Discussions: Turning Arguments into Conversations

Structured conflict discussions are like having a roadmap when you're lost in a new city. They're not about stifling spontaneity but about creating a safe space where both partners can express their views without the conversation spiraling into a shouting match. Imagine trying to discuss a sensitive topic, and before you know it, you're both yelling and not listening. A framework helps manage these conflicts by providing a structured environment. This approach prevents escalation, fostering mutual understanding instead. It's like having rules for a fair game—everyone knows what to expect, making it easier to play without fouls.

So, how do you structure these discussions effectively? Start with a calm and neutral tone, avoiding the ever-discouraging "We need to talk." This phrase alone can kill any hope of having a positive conversation. To set the stage for a productive discussion rather than a heated argument, it's crucial to keep emotions in check right from the get-go. Next, take turns speaking without interruption. This isn't just polite; it ensures that each person can share their perspective fully. Interruptions often lead to misunderstandings and frustration, so give each other the floor one at a time. Focus on one issue at a time. It's easy to let a discussion about dirty dishes morph into an argument about who forgot the anniversary. Keeping the conversation on track helps address the real issue without getting sidetracked. Finally, summarize and validate each other's points. Before moving on, make sure you've understood what your partner is saying. A simple "So, what I hear you saying is..." "can go a long way in ensuring clarity and mutual understanding.

Active listening plays a pivotal role in structured discussions. It's more than just hearing the words; it's about genuinely listening to each other. Reflective listening techniques can be incredibly effective. This means echoing what your partner has said to show you've understood. For instance, if your partner says, "I feel overwhelmed with the housework," you might respond, "It sounds like you're feeling stressed about all the chores." This shows you're not just hearing but understanding. Asking clarifying questions is also essential. Don't hesitate to ask for more information if something is unclear. Questions like, "Can you explain what you mean by that?" or "How did that make you feel?" can help deepen understanding and prevent miscommunication.

Let's bring this to life with a real-life example. Suppose you and your partner often argue about household chores. One of you feels like you're doing all the work, while the other feels overwhelmed with different responsibilities. Using the structured discussion framework, you start with a calm tone. One partner begins by expressing their feelings without interruption. "I feel overwhelmed because I feel like I'm handling most of the chores." The other partner listens, summarizes, and validates: "I hear you saying you're feeling overwhelmed and burdened with the chores. Is that right?" This simple act of reflecting and validating can defuse tension and make the conversation more productive.

To practice, try role-playing scenarios using this framework. Let's say the disagreement is about finances this time. One partner might start by saying, "I feel stressed about our budget because we seem to be overspending." The other listens, then reflects and validates: "So, you're feeling stressed because you think we're spending too much. Can we talk more about that?" By practicing these scenarios, you'll get more comfortable with the structure and find it easier to use in real-life situations.

Structured conflict discussions are about turning arguments into conversations. They provide a safe environment for both partners to express their views, preventing escalation and fostering mutual understanding. You can navigate conflicts more effectively by following a clear framework—starting with a calm tone, taking turns speaking, focusing on one issue at a time, and summarizing each other's points. Active listening, reflective techniques, and asking clarifying questions are crucial components. With practice, you'll find that structured discussions become a natural and effective way to resolve conflicts, bringing you closer together rather than driving you apart.

3.3 Emotional Intelligence: Understanding and Managing Emotions

Emotional intelligence, often abbreviated as EQ, is like having a superpower in your relationship toolkit. It's all about recognizing and understanding your own emotions, empathizing with your partner's feelings, and managing emotions constructively. Imagine navigating tricky emotional waters without capsizing—sounds good, right? Emotional intelligence is crucial for healthy relationships because it helps you connect more deeply, fostering understanding and reducing conflicts. Recognizing your own emotions means you can identify when you're upset or stressed before it spirals into a full-blown argument. Empathy allows you to tune into your partner's emotional state, creating a supportive and nurturing environment. Managing emotions constructively means handling disagreements without letting anger or frustration take the wheel.

Breaking down the components of emotional intelligence helps make it more actionable. First up is self-awareness. This is about understanding your emotional triggers. Maybe you get irritated when your partner leaves dishes in the sink, or perhaps you feel anxious when plans change suddenly. Knowing these triggers helps you manage your reactions better. Self-regulation is next. It's about keeping your emotions in check. Instead of snapping when annoyed, you take a deep breath and respond calmly. Motivation involves using your emotions to achieve positive outcomes. If you're stressed, channel that energy into solving the problem rather than letting it fester. Empathy is about connecting with your partner's emotions. When they're upset, you don't just see it; you feel it. This connection fosters a more profound bond and helps in resolving conflicts. Lastly, social skills are about communicating and resolving conflicts effectively. It's knowing how to express your feelings clearly and listen to your partner's perspective.

Developing emotional intelligence doesn't happen overnight, but you can get there with practice. Start with journaling to identify and understand your emotional responses. Write down situations that triggered strong emotions and reflect on why you felt that way. This practice helps you become more aware of your emotional landscape. Mindfulness and meditation practices are excellent for emotional regulation. Taking a few minutes each day to meditate can help you stay centered and calm, making it easier to handle emotional stress.

Empathy-building exercises are also valuable. Try putting yourself in your partner's shoes. Imagine how you would feel in their situation if they were upset about something. This practice can deepen your empathy and improve your emotional connection.

Real-life examples can show how powerful emotional intelligence can be. Take the case of Sarah and Mike. They struggled to communicate after Mike lost his job. Sarah felt the financial pressure, while Mike felt like a failure. Instead of letting these emotions drive a wedge between them, they worked on their emotional intelligence. Sarah practiced empathy, trying to understand Mike's feelings of inadequacy. Mike worked on self-awareness, recognizing his emotional triggers. They both used self-regulation techniques to keep their emotions in check during discussions. Over time, their relationship improved as they learned to navigate this significant life change together.

Another couple, Jane and Paul, found that enhancing their emotional intelligence helped them manage everyday stressors more effectively. Jane started journaling to identify what overwhelmed her, while Paul practiced mindfulness to stay calm under pressure. They also engaged in empathy-building exercises, like discussing how they would feel in each other's situations. These practices helped them better understand and support each other, reducing conflicts and strengthening their bond.

Emotional intelligence is like a secret weapon for building a robust and resilient relationship. By recognizing and understanding your own emotions, empathizing with your partner's feelings, and managing emotions constructively, you can easily navigate the ups and downs of marriage. Self-awareness, self-regulation, motivation, empathy, and social skills are the critical components of EQ, each playing a crucial role in fostering a healthy relationship. Practical strategies like journaling, mindfulness, and empathy-building exercises can help you enhance your emotional intelligence. And as Sarah, Mike, Jane, and Paul's stories show, the benefits are well worth the effort.

3.4 Empathy vs. Sympathy: Strengthening Emotional Connections

Imagine you've had a terrible day. You come home and tell your partner about it. They say, "Wow, that sucks. I'm sorry you're going through that." That's sympathy, and while it's nice, it doesn't make you feel understood. Imagine your partner saying, "I can't believe how tough that must have been for you. I remember feeling similarly overwhelmed when I was in a similar situation." That's empathy. The key difference here is that empathy involves understanding and sharing another's partner's feelings, while sympathy involves feeling pity or sorrow for someone else's misfortune. This distinction is crucial because empathy fosters a deeper emotional connection and helps build stronger relationships. When you empathize, you're not just acknowledging your partner's feelings; you're connecting with them on an emotional level, which can be incredibly powerful in strengthening your bond.

Empathy has a profound impact on relationships. It creates a deeper emotional connection by showing your partner that you genuinely understand what they're going through. This understanding enhances mutual trust and makes it easier to resolve conflicts. When your partner feels understood, they're more likely to open up and share their feelings, leading to a more intimate and trusting relationship. Imagine a scenario where your partner is upset about a work issue. Instead of just saying, "I'm sorry you're stressed," you might say, "I can see how this project is weighing on you, especially with the tight deadlines. How can I support you?" This response shows empathy and can transform a potentially negative interaction into a positive one, strengthening your relationship.

Developing empathy takes practice, but it's entirely doable with some actionable steps. Start with active listening and reflective responses. When your partner speaks, give them your full attention and send back what you've heard to ensure you understand. For instance, if they say, "I'm feeling overwhelmed with everything on my plate," you might respond, "It sounds like you're feeling stressed with all your responsibilities." This simple act of mirroring shows you're genuinely listening and trying to understand their feelings. Practicing perspective-taking is another effective technique. Try to put yourself in your partner's shoes and imagine how they're feeling. This can help you develop a more in-depth understanding of their emotions and respond more empathetically.

Engaging in empathy-building exercises can also be incredibly beneficial. One effective exercise is "empathy mapping." This involves sitting down with your partner and discussing a recent experience from both perspectives. Take turns sharing how you felt during the experience and what you perceived the other person was feeling. This exercise helps you see things from each other's point of view and enhances your ability to empathize. Another helpful practice is "daily empathy check-ins." Set aside a few minutes each day to discuss your feelings and experiences. Ask each other questions like, "How are you feeling today?" or "What was the best and worst part of your day?" These check-ins create a regular habit of sharing and understanding each other's emotions, fostering a deeper connection.

Exercise: Practicing Empathy

8. Empathy Mapping: Sit down with your partner and discuss a recent experience from both perspectives. Take turns sharing how you felt and what you perceived the other person was feeling.

9. Daily Empathy Check-Ins: Set aside a few minutes each day to discuss your feelings and experiences. Ask questions like, "How are you feeling today?" or "What was the best and worst part of your day?" With today's busy lifestyles, makingwould never time to work on this may sound impossible. Try talking while cooking or putting away the laundry.

Focusing on empathy rather than sympathy can help you build stronger emotional connections with your partner. Empathy involves understanding and sharing another's feelings, which creates a deeper emotional bond and enhances mutual trust. Practicing active listening, perspective-taking, and engaging in empathy-building exercises can help you become a more empathetic partner. With empathy, you can navigate conflicts more effectively and create a more supportive and understanding relationship.

My father died at 52 of an undiagnosed genetic "thing" in his heart when I was 10, so I don't remember the specifics of mom and dad's relationship. I do recall laughter and fun, plenty of trips and mini vacations, and seldom arguments. All that changed when we left the USA to live with Mom's family. It was the patriarchy at its worst. There was nothing desirable about marriage, and at 15, I decided I was never going to do it. Somehow, real life and the banana republic society I was living in caught me in its web, and just like that, I was married at 18. It wasn't until I returned to the States that my disdain for this institution would solidify. I came to the disappointing conclusion that the patriarchy, although less confining, was alive and well here too.

This little walk down memory lane brings me directly to the steps of the next topic. The emotional baggage of my formative years would haunt me for decades. My point here is that you must love yourself before you can love, or at least share your life with, someone else. You need to know who you are and where your boundaries, goals, and dreams are. So, like Alice in Wonderland, "If you don't know where you are going, it doesn't matter what path you take." However, this is a topic for another book.

3.5 Dealing with Emotional Baggage: Healing from Past Hurts

This is a tough subject for me because I have been carrying a lot of baggage, and I am still working on it. The first marriage was a doozy; more issues were involved there than a subscription to Time Magazine, and much still lingers. My second mainly was on me; however, he was one of those Stoic guys who doesn't do feelings often and likes to ignore things until they go away. Getting diagnosed with Postpartum Depression and later with Bipolar disorder did not help. My progress on the 3rd try is better, but I am still a long way away from ideal.

Emotional baggage—just the term itself feels heavy, doesn't it? It's that invisible backpack filled with past traumas, unresolved issues, and negative experiences that we all carry around, whether we realize it or not. In a marriage, this baggage can sneakily influence your interactions and reactions. Maybe you've got trust issues from a previous relationship or childhood trauma that makes you fear intimacy. These past hurts can manifest in various ways, like being overly suspicious, distant, or even excessively clingy. They act like unseen forces, shaping how you respond to your partner and how you perceive their actions. This is why some couples fall into rabbit holes that have nothing to do with the issue at hand. Staying mindful in the moment will help you stay within the framework of the present and allow you to stop going after the rabbit.

Addressing emotional baggage is crucial because, if left unchecked, it can act like a ticking time bomb in your relationship. I'm not advocating for anyone to bear all their dirty laundry out for all to see, but a general idea of what has been may be helpful in the future. Confronting and healing from past hurts prevent these issues from poisoning your present dynamics. It promotes emotional healing and growth, allowing you to build a healthier, more resilient relationship. Imagine trying to build a house on a shaky foundation—it's bound to collapse at some point. The same goes for relationships. Dealing with your emotional baggage ensures your relationship has a stable foundation, capable of weathering life's storms.

So, how do you deal with this emotional baggage? One effective strategy is seeking professional help, such as therapy or counseling. A trained therapist can help you unpack those old issues, understand their impact on your current behavior, and develop coping strategies. Journaling and self-reflection exercises are also invaluable. Writing down your thoughts and feelings can help you identify patterns and triggers, making you more aware of how your past affects your present. It's like shining a flashlight into the dark corners of your mind, bringing hidden issues to light. While this can be unpleasant, it is necessary to be able to focus on what matters now. You can start with the latest self-help book of your choice and work up to professional help as your finances and comfort level allow.

Open and honest communication with your partner is another critical strategy. Share your experiences and how they affected you. This transparency fosters understanding and empathy, allowing your partner to support you better. For instance, if you have trust issues due to a past betrayal, explaining this to your partner helps them understand your reactions and work with you to build trust. It's not about dumping your baggage on them, but about making them aware—heads up! So to speak—so that you can work through it together.

Real-life examples can be incredibly inspiring. Take the case of Lisa and Tom. Lisa had significant trust issues due to a past betrayal, which caused constant friction in their marriage. They decided to seek couples counseling, where they learned techniques to rebuild trust and communicate more effectively. Over time, Lisa's trust issues diminished, and their relationship grew stronger. Another example is Bryan, who had childhood trauma that made him fear intimacy. Through therapy and open communication with his partner, he gradually healed and built a more intimate, loving relationship.

These success stories show that dealing with emotional baggage is not only possible but also transformative. It's about acknowledging your past, understanding its impact, and taking steps to heal. This process creates a stronger, more resilient relationship where both partners feel understood and supported. Emotional baggage might seem like a heavy load, but with the right tools and support, you can lighten the load and build a healthier, happier relationship.

Chapter 4:
Rebuilding and Maintaining Trust

Picture this: You're making your morning coffee, and you realize you're out of your favorite creamer. Frustrating, right? Now, multiply that frustration by a thousand, and you might start to grasp the feeling of broken trust in a relationship. Trust is like that creamer—it's essential, and when it's gone, everything feels off. Rebuilding trust isn't just about patching things up; it's about actively engaging in activities designed to strengthen and restore that foundation.

4.1 Trust-Building Activities: Steps Towards Forgiveness

Trust-building activities are the lifeline for any relationship in need of repair. Think of them as the essential maintenance tasks that keep your relationship running smoothly. One powerful exercise is the trust walk, where one partner is blindfolded and guided by the other. This activity is a beautiful metaphor for trust—literally putting your faith in your partner to lead you safely. It can be a fun way to demonstrate reliance and build a deeper connection.

Another fantastic trust-building activity is mutual goal setting. Working together to achieve shared objectives creates a sense of partnership and mutual investment. Whether planning a vacation, saving for a house, or simply deciding to cook healthier meals, setting and achieving goals together fosters a sense of teamwork and shared purpose. This mutual effort can help rebuild trust as you work towards common goals, showing that you're both committed to the relationship.

But trust-building doesn't stop there. A variety of activities can help you and your partner reconnect and rebuild trust. Daily check-ins are a great start. Setting aside time each day to discuss feelings and concerns can keep communication lines open and prevent misunderstandings from festering. It's about making a habit of checking in with each other, ensuring that you're both on the same page emotionally.

Trust falls might sound like a corporate team-building cliché, but they can be incredibly effective. This physical exercise reinforces reliance on each other. When you fall backward, trusting your partner to catch you, it's a tangible demonstration of faith in each other's support. It's simple but powerful in reinforcing the idea that you've got each other's backs.

Engaging in shared hobbies is another excellent trust-building exercise. Whether hiking, cooking, or binge-watching a favorite show, spending quality time together doing something you both enjoy can strengthen your bond. These shared experiences create positive memories and reinforce the idea that you're a team, working together and enjoying life's moments.

Forgiveness plays a crucial role in rebuilding trust. Understanding the difference between forgiveness and forgetting is essential. Forgiveness is about letting go of resentment and moving forward while forgetting, which implies erasing the past, which isn't always possible or healthy. Genuine forgiveness involves acknowledging the hurt and choosing to let it go, making a conscious decision to move forward without holding past mistakes over each other's heads.

Steps to genuinely forgive a partner's past mistakes involve several vital actions. First, acknowledge the hurt caused by the mistake. This means openly discussing the pain and understanding its impact on the relationship. Next, take responsibility for your actions. The person who made the mistake must genuinely apologize and accept their role in the issue. Then, both partners need to work on rebuilding trust through consistent actions and open communication. It's a process that takes time and effort from both sides.

Other real-life examples are the story of Jenna and Mike, a couple who overcame infidelity through daily check-ins and trust walks. After Mike's affair, they committed to rebuilding their relationship. They started with daily check-ins to discuss their feelings and progress. They also incorporated trust walks into their routine, using the exercise as a way to rebuild their connection. Over time, these activities helped them move past the betrayal and strengthen their bond. Sarah and Tom strengthened their bond by pursuing a shared hobby. They both loved painting but had never done it together. After a rough patch in their marriage, they decided to take a painting class together. This shared activity gave them a new way to connect and communicate, helping them rebuild trust and enjoy each other's company.

Trust-building activities are essential for any couple looking to rebuild and maintain trust. From trust walks and mutual goal setting to daily check-ins, trust falls, and shared hobbies; these activities create opportunities for connection and reassurance. Forgiveness is vital to this process, involving genuine acknowledgment of hurt and a commitment to moving forward. Real-life examples, like those of Jenna and Mike or Sarah and Tom, show that with dedication and effort, trust can be rebuilt, leading to more robust, more resilient relationships.

4.2 Apology Frameworks: Saying "Sorry" with impact

Have you ever had one of those apologies that felt more like a slap in the face than a balm for the soul? Yeah, we've all been there. A sincere apology is crucial for rebuilding trust because it acknowledges the hurt caused and takes responsibility for its actions. It's not just about saying "sorry" but about genuinely understanding the impact of your actions and showing a commitment to change. When you acknowledge the hurt, you tell your partner their feelings matter. It's like saying, "I see you, I hear you, and I understand the pain I've caused." Taking responsibility means owning up to your mistakes without shifting the blame. It shows maturity and integrity, signaling you're committed to making things right.

So, how do you deliver an apology that actually makes a difference? Enter the apology frameworks. These structured approaches can help you say sorry in a way that resonates and rebuilds trust. One effective method is the 4 R's: Recognize, Regret, Responsibility, and Remedy. First, recognize what you did wrong. Next, express genuine regret for the pain you caused. Then, take responsibility for your actions without any excuses. Finally, offer a remedy—a plan to make amends and avoid repeating the mistake. For example, you might say, "I recognize that my actions hurt you, and I deeply regret causing you pain. I take full responsibility and will make amends by being more considerate in the future."

Another practical framework is the 3 A's: Acknowledge, Apologize, and Amend. This approach is more straightforward but equally effective. Start by acknowledging the mistake and its impact. Then, offer a heartfelt apology. Finally, outline the steps you'll take to amend the situation. For instance, "I acknowledge that I've been neglecting our time together, and I'm truly sorry. I'll make it a priority to spend more quality time with you."

However, even the best frameworks can fall flat if you stumble into common pitfalls. One major mistake is offering a conditional apology, like "I'm sorry if you felt hurt." This type of apology shifts the blame onto the person who's hurt, implying that their feelings are the problem rather than your actions. Another pitfall is following the apology with justifications. Saying, "I'm sorry, but I was very stressed," undermines the sincerity of your apology by making it sound like an excuse. Avoid these traps by sticking to the frameworks and focusing on the hurt caused rather than your reasons for causing it.

Practice is key to getting better at delivering sincere apologies. Role-playing different scenarios requiring an apology can be incredibly helpful. Imagine a situation where you forgot an important date, like your partner's birthday. Practice delivering an apology using the 4 R's or the 3 A's, focusing on acknowledging the hurt, expressing regret, taking responsibility, and outlining a plan to make amends. This exercise helps you get comfortable with the frameworks and ensures that your apologies come from a place of genuine understanding and remorse. Here is a brief overview of each:

Four Rs of Apologizing:

10. Regret: Express genuine remorse for the mistake or wrongdoing. Show that you understand and feel sorry for the hurt or inconvenience caused.

11. Responsibility: Acknowledge your role in the situation. Accept full responsibility for your actions and avoid deflecting blame.

12. Repair: Take action to fix the issue or make amends. This might involve offering compensation, correcting the mistake, or taking steps to prevent a recurrence.

13. Renewal: Commit to personal or behavioral changes to prevent the same issue from happening again. This demonstrates that you've learned from the experience and are dedicated to improving.

3 A's of Apologizing:

14. Acknowledge: Recognize and admit what went wrong. This involves understanding and articulating the specific issue or harm caused.

15. Apologize: Offer a sincere apology. Clearly express regret and take responsibility for your actions.

16. Amend: Make efforts to remedy the situation. This includes taking concrete steps to address the harm and prevent future issues.

Another practical activity is writing "apology letters" to each other. This exercise allows you to take the time to reflect on your actions and articulate your apology thoughtfully. Writing it down can help you organize your thoughts and ensure that your apology covers all the necessary elements. Plus, a written apology can serve as a tangible reminder of your commitment to change.

Exercise: Writing Apology Letters

17. Reflect on a recent mistake or issue in your relationship.

18. Write a detailed apology letter to your partner using either the 4 R's or the 3 A's framework.

19. Exchange letters and discuss them, focusing on the emotions and commitments expressed.

By incorporating these frameworks and practices, you can deliver apologies that genuinely resonate and help rebuild trust. A sincere apology isn't just a quick fix; it's a powerful tool for healing and strengthening your relationship. So, the next time you need to apologize, do it with impact and watch how it transforms your connection. A friend of Bill's has a suggestion, "make amends wherever possible, except when to do so would injure them or others." Recognize, however, that some doors are best left closed.

4.3 Transparency and Honesty: Foundations of Trust

Imagine you're on a road trip, but your partner is holding the map and not sharing the directions. Frustrating, right? That's what a lack of transparency and honesty feels like in a relationship. Transparency means being open about your actions and intentions. It's about not hiding things, whether it's your plans for the weekend or how you're feeling about a tough day at work. Honesty, on the other hand, involves sharing your thoughts and feelings truthfully. Together, these qualities form the cornerstone of trust. When you're transparent and honest, you're telling your partner, "I trust you enough to be open with you," and that's a big deal.

Maintaining transparency and honesty can have a profoundly positive impact on your relationship. First off, it creates a safe and secure environment where both partners feel valued and understood. When you're open about your actions and intentions, you remove the guesswork. Your partner doesn't have to play detective, wondering what you're up to or how you're feeling. This openness fosters emotional intimacy and connection, making navigating life's ups and downs easier. Imagine coming home after a long day and being able to share your thoughts openly without fear of judgment. This level of honesty deepens your bond and strengthens your relationship's foundation.

Now, how do you foster these qualities in your relationship? One effective strategy is to schedule "honesty hours." This is a dedicated time when you and your partner share openly about your day, your feelings, and any concerns you might have. During honesty hours, the goal is to listen without judgment and to speak without holding back. It's about creating a safe space for open dialogue. Another powerful approach is adopting a no-secrets policy. This means agreeing to share all relevant information with each other. Whether it's financial details, work-related stress, or personal feelings, keeping no secrets ensures that both partners are always in the loop. For example, during honesty hours, you might discuss your day openly and without judgment, sharing both the highs and the lows. This regular practice can build a habit of transparency and make it easier to maintain honesty in everyday interactions.

Real-life examples can beautifully illustrate the power of transparency and honesty. Take the story of Elliot and Sandra, who overcame financial secrecy by adopting a no-secrets policy. Sam had been hiding some financial troubles, fearing Lisa's reaction. When the truth came out, it caused a significant rift. They decided to implement a no-secrets policy, openly discussing their finances and working together to resolve the issues. This transparency helped them overcome the immediate problem and strengthened their trust in each other. Another couple, John and Emily, strengthened their relationship through regular honesty hours. They set aside time each evening to talk about their day and share their thoughts. This practice helped them stay connected and understand each other better, reducing conflicts and increasing their emotional intimacy.

Transparency and honesty are foundational for trust because they eliminate the need for guesswork and create a safe environment for open communication. Being open about your actions and intentions and honestly sharing your thoughts and feelings can significantly enhance your relationship dynamics. Strategies like regularly scheduled honesty hours and adopting a no-secret policy can help cultivate these qualities. Real-life examples, like those of Sam and Lisa or John and Emily, demonstrate that with commitment and effort, maintaining transparency and honesty can lead to more robust, more fulfilling relationships.

4.4 Consistent Actions: Building Trust Over Time

Trust isn't rebuilt overnight; it's a marathon, not a sprint. Consistency is the bedrock of trust. Imagine you're trying to rebuild a crumbling wall. Each consistent action is a brick, laid carefully and sturdily to reconstruct that wall of trust. Demonstrating reliability and dependability is crucial. When you consistently follow through on what you say you'll do, it sends a powerful message: "You can count on me." This regular, trustworthy behavior reinforces trust over time, creating a solid foundation that can withstand future challenges.

Let's talk about specific behaviors that can help reinforce trust. Keeping promises and commitments is a big one. If you say you'll pick up groceries on your way home, do it. These small acts of reliability add up, showing your partner that your word is golden. Being punctual and reliable is another essential aspect. If you agree to meet at 7 PM for dinner, be there on time. It's not just about the clock; it's about showing respect for your partner's time and trust in your dependability. Consistently following through on agreed-upon plans, no matter how small, builds a track record of reliability. Over time, this record becomes a testament to your commitment and trustworthiness.

Inconsistency, however, is the arch-nemesis of trust. Broken promises can have a devastating impact, creating a ripple effect of doubt and insecurity. Imagine promising to attend a significant event with your partner and bailing at the last minute. It's like kicking a hole in that wall you're trying to rebuild. Unpredictability can lead to insecurity, making your partner question your reliability and commitment. When your actions are inconsistent, it sends mixed signals, causing confusion and eroding trust. It's like trying to build on quicksand; nothing stable can come of it.

To practice consistency, consider creating a "trust journal." This isn't about keeping tabs on each other but about tracking your consistent actions. Write down the commitments you make and note when you follow through. Reflecting on these entries can help reinforce the importance of reliability and show tangible progress. Another practical activity is setting and achieving small daily goals together. These goals don't have to be monumental; they can be as simple as committing to a daily walk or cooking dinner together once a week. The key is to follow through consistently, building a habit of reliability. This list is for personal growth, NOT keeping score.

Role-playing scenarios that require consistent follow-through can also be beneficial. Imagine a situation where you've promised to support your partner in a new hobby. Practice how you'll keep that promise, from setting reminders to actively participating. This exercise can help you anticipate challenges and develop strategies to stay consistent. It's all about reinforcing the habit of following through, making it second nature.

Exercise: Practicing Consistency

20. Create a Trust Journal: Track your commitments and follow-through actions. Reflect on your progress regularly.

21. Set Small Daily Goals: Achieve these goals together, reinforcing the habit of reliability.

22. Role-Playing Scenarios: Practice keeping promises in various situations to build consistency.

Consistency isn't about grand gestures; it's about the small, everyday actions that show your partner they can rely on you. You build a solid foundation of trust by focusing on keeping promises, being punctual, and following through on plans. Inconsistent behavior, on the other hand, can undermine this foundation, creating doubt and insecurity. Practical exercises like trust journals, setting daily goals, and role-playing can help you develop the habit of consistency. These actions, over time, will reinforce trust and create a reliable, dependable relationship.

4.5 Rebuilding Trust After Betrayal: Real-Life Success Stories

Trust is a fragile thing, often shattered by betrayal but not beyond repair. Let's talk about real-life stories of couples who faced significant breaches of trust and came out stronger on the other side. Take, for example, the story of Jake and Lisa. After Jake's infidelity, their marriage was hanging by a thread. Both were engulfed in a storm of emotions—pain, anger, and deep sadness. But they chose to fight for their relationship. They sought professional help through therapy, which provided a safe space to express their feelings and fears. Therapy helped them understand the underlying issues that led to the betrayal and offered tools to rebuild their relationship. They also engaged in trust-building activities, like spending quality time together and maintaining open communication. Over time, their efforts paid off, and they rebuilt a stronger, more honest relationship.

Another compelling story is that of Tom and Emily, who faced a different kind of betrayal—financial deception. Tom had been hiding significant debt from Emily, fearing her reaction. When the truth came out, Emily was devastated. They sought counseling, which helped them navigate the complex emotions and rebuild their financial trust. They also took practical steps like creating a transparent budget and setting financial goals together. Engaging in these activities helped them rebuild their trust and strengthened their partnership. Their journey was filled with emotional ups and downs, but their commitment to transparency and honesty ultimately saved their relationship.

The emotional journey of rebuilding trust is not a straight path. It's filled with initial pain and anger but also moments of healing and forgiveness. The initial phase is often the hardest, as both partners grapple with intense emotions. The betrayed partner feels hurt and betrayed, while the betrayer grapples with guilt and shame. This phase requires a lot of patience and understanding. Gradually, with consistent effort and open communication, the wounds begin to heal. Forgiveness starts to take root, not as a way to forget the past, but as a way to move forward. It's a process that requires time, effort, and a willingness to rebuild the relationship one step at a time.

Hope and motivation are crucial during this rebuilding phase. It's important to remember that rebuilding trust is possible with dedication and effort. Consider the encouraging words of Sarah, who rebuilt her marriage after her partner's infidelity: "It wasn't easy, but we chose to believe in each other and our love. Trust isn't given; it's earned, and we worked hard to earn it back." Practical advice from couples who've been through this process can be invaluable. They often emphasize the importance of patience, open communication, and professional help. Remember, rebuilding trust is not about erasing the past but about creating a new, stronger foundation for the future.

So, whether you're dealing with infidelity, financial betrayal, or any other breach of trust, know that it's possible to rebuild and come out stronger. Trust can be rebuilt, and relationships can thrive again with the right tools and a lot of heart.

Chapter 5:
Intimacy: Emotional and Physical Connection

Have you ever noticed how easy it is to become roommates instead of romantic partners? You know that moment when you're sitting on the couch together, but both of you are engrossed in your phones, barely exchanging a word? It's a slippery slope from "Can't keep my hands off you" to "Can you grab some milk on your way home?" Intimacy isn't just a given; it's something you have to nurture. And guess what? Regular date nights are one of the best ways to keep that spark alive. They're like those little oil changes that keep your relationship engine running smoothly.

5.1 Weekly Date Nights: Keeping the Spark Alive

Let's face it: life is busy. It's easy to let your relationship take a back seat between work, family, and all those never-ending to-do lists. But setting aside time for regular date nights is crucial for maintaining intimacy. Date nights provide a golden opportunity to reconnect away from daily stresses, giving you both a chance to focus on each other. It's like hitting the pause button on life's chaos and dedicating time to just be together. Whether you're married, engaged, or in a relationship, these moments of connection help keep the romance and excitement alive. Think of it as a mini-vacation for your relationship, a chance to recharge and remember why you chose each other in the first place.

Now, let's discuss spicing things up with creative and varied date night ideas. Themed dinner nights at home can be a blast. Imagine transforming your dining room into a little Italian bistro, complete with homemade pasta and a bottle of wine. Or how about a sushi night where you both try your hand at rolling sushi? It's fun, interactive, and delicious. Outdoor activities like hiking or picnicking offer a great way to enjoy nature while spending quality time together. Pack a picnic basket with your favorite snacks and head to a nearby park for a relaxing afternoon. If you're more into cultural experiences, attending events such as theater performances or concerts can be a fantastic way to bond over shared interests. Plus, dressing up for a night out adds a touch of glamor and excitement.

The benefits of planning and anticipation are often overlooked but incredibly impactful. The process of planning a date night builds excitement and anticipation leading up to the event. It's like looking forward to a mini-adventure together. This anticipation can reignite those butterflies you felt in the early stages of your relationship. Moreover, planning shows effort and thoughtfulness in keeping the relationship vibrant. It's a way of saying, "You're important to me, and I enjoy spending time with you." Whether it's a simple movie night or an elaborate dinner, the act of planning itself adds an extra layer of intimacy.

But how do you ensure date nights happen regularly despite busy schedules? First, schedule them in advance on a shared calendar. Treat date nights like any other important appointment. By marking them on the calendar, you're making a commitment to each other, ensuring that other plans don't get in the way. Setting ground rules to avoid distractions is also key. No phones, no work talk—just the two of you focusing on each other. For example, you could set a recurring date night on the same day each week to create a routine. Maybe Friday nights become your dedicated time to unwind and connect, giving you both something to look forward to at the end of the week.

Exercise: Planning Your Next Date Night

23. Choose a Theme: Decide on a theme for your next date night, whether it's a cultural cuisine, an outdoor adventure, or attending a special event.

24. Set a Date: Mark the date on your shared calendar and commit to it.

25. Plan Together: Discuss the details together, from the menu to the activities, building anticipation and excitement.

26. Unplug: Set ground rules to avoid distractions and focus on each other.

By prioritizing date nights, you're investing in your relationship's long-term health and happiness. Regularly setting aside time to reconnect helps maintain intimacy, keeps the romance alive, and ensures that you both feel valued and appreciated. So, go ahead and plan that themed dinner night, hike, or concert. Your relationship will thank you for it.

5.2 Love Language Quizzes: Understanding Your Partner's Needs

Have you ever felt like you're speaking a different language than your partner, even though you're both technically speaking English? Sometimes it feels like you're saying, "I love you," but what they hear is, "I forgot to take out the trash." This is where the concept of love languages comes into play. Love languages, a term coined by Dr. Gary Chapman, are essentially the different ways people express and receive love. There are five of them: words of affirmation, acts of service, receiving gifts, quality time, and physical touch. Understanding these love languages is crucial for intimacy because it helps you connect with your partner in a way that resonates most deeply with them. Think of it as having a personalized love manual for your relationship.

Words of affirmation are about verbal expressions of love and appreciation. If this is your partner's love language, they thrive on compliments and words of encouragement. On the other hand, acts of service involve doing things for your partner to show you care—like cooking dinner or running errands. Receiving gifts isn't just about materialism; it's about the thoughtfulness behind the gift. Quality time means giving your partner your undivided attention, while physical touch involves everything from holding hands to hugging. Each love language influences how we give and receive love, and understanding your partner's primary love language can transform your relationship. It's like having the right key to unlock a deeper level of connection.

So, how do you figure out your and your partner's love languages? One way is through love language quizzes. These are designed to help couples identify their own and each other's love languages. You can find plenty of online quizzes or printable questionnaires that make this process easy and fun. Self-reflection exercises are also valuable in understanding personal preferences. Take some time to think about what makes you feel most loved and appreciated. Is it when your partner says something kind, does something helpful, gives you a thoughtful gift, spends quality time with you, or shows affection through touch? Reflecting on these questions can provide insights into your love language.

Once you've identified your love languages, consistently speaking and applying this knowledge in daily life is the next step. Tailoring your actions and expressions of love to match your partner's love language can significantly enhance your relationship. For example, if your partner's love language is acts of service, they might appreciate help with household chores. You could take on a task they usually handle, like doing the laundry or cooking dinner, to show your love in a way that speaks to them. If their love language is words of affirmation, daily affirmations can go a long way. Telling them how much you appreciate them or acknowledging something they did well can make them feel loved and valued.

For those whose love language is quality time, planning activities that allow you to spend undivided time together is key. This could be as simple as watching a movie together, going for a walk, or having a meaningful conversation without distractions. Creating a "love language calendar" can be a fun and effective way to ensure you're consistently speaking each other's love language. This calendar could include daily or weekly activities tailored to each other's love languages, like planning a special outing for quality time or setting reminders to give compliments for words of affirmation.

Exercise: Discovering and Practicing Love Languages

27. Love Language Quizzes: Take an online quiz or use a printable questionnaire to discover your and your partner's love languages.

28. Self-Reflection: Spend some time reflecting on what makes you feel most loved and appreciated.

29. Love Language Calendar: Create a calendar with daily or weekly activities tailored to each other's love languages.

Understanding and practicing each other's love languages can create a more intimate and fulfilling relationship. It's about making an effort to speak your partner's love language, even if it doesn't come naturally to you. The payoff is a deeper connection and a stronger bond built on mutual understanding and appreciation.

5.3 Physical Intimacy: Beyond the Bedroom

When we mention physical intimacy, most people immediately think of sex. But physical intimacy is so much more than just what happens between the sheets. It includes affectionate touch, cuddling, holding hands, and all those little non-sexual moments of physical closeness that help maintain an emotional connection. Think about it: a simple touch on the arm, a hug when you walk in the door, or holding hands while watching TV—all these acts create a physical bond that speaks volumes, even when words fail. These small gestures can make you feel loved, valued, and connected.

Non-sexual physical intimacy has a myriad of benefits. For starters, it reduces stress and promotes feelings of safety and comfort. There's something incredibly soothing about a hug at the end of a long day or resting your head on your partner's shoulder. These touches activate the release of oxytocin, often called the "love hormone," which helps lower stress levels and fosters a sense of well-being. Additionally, non-sexual touch reinforces emotional connection and trust. When you reach out to hold your partner's hand, it's a silent way of saying, "I'm here for you." These small, everyday gestures build a strong foundation for your relationship, making it easier to weather the storms together.

Incorporating physical intimacy into your daily life doesn't have to be complicated. Morning and bedtime rituals involving touch can set the tone for a connected day and a restful night. Imagine starting your day with a simple cuddle in bed or ending it with a goodnight kiss. These rituals create moments of connection that bookend your day, making you feel closer to each other. Holding hands or hugging frequently throughout the day is another easy way to maintain physical closeness. It's remarkable how a quick hug or holding hands while walking can make you feel more connected.

One practical tip is to create a "touch calendar" where you set reminders for daily acts of physical affection. It might sound a bit mechanical, but it can be incredibly effective, especially if you find that your busy lives often push physical closeness to the back burner. For example, you could set a reminder to give your partner a hug when they get home or to hold hands during your evening walk. These little moments add up, creating a tapestry of connection that strengthens your bond.

To enhance physical intimacy further, try engaging in activities that require physical closeness and collaboration. Partner yoga or couples' massage can be fantastic ways to deepen your physical connection. Partner yoga involves practicing poses that require mutual support, balance, and synchronization. It's not just about physical exercise but also about moving in harmony with your partner, creating a deeper sense of unity. Couples' massage, whether you're giving or receiving, fosters a sense of care and relaxation. It's a wonderful way to show love through touch, helping both of you unwind and feel cherished.

Slow dancing to your favorite music at home is another beautiful way to connect physically. Turn on a slow song, dim the lights, and just dance together in your living room. It's intimate and romantic and doesn't require any special skills or elaborate planning. The simple act of swaying together, feeling each other's heartbeat, can create a powerful moment of connection. These unscripted, spontaneous moments often leave the most lasting impressions.

Exercise: Enhancing Physical Intimacy

30. Partner Yoga: Find a partner yoga video online and practice together. Focus on poses that require collaboration and physical support.

31. Couples' Massage: Take turns giving each other a massage. Use this time to relax and connect through touch.

32. Slow Dancing: Pick a favorite song and dance together at home. Enjoy the closeness and the simple joy of moving together.

Physical intimacy goes beyond the bedroom and encompasses all those little touches and gestures that keep you connected. Incorporating these moments into your daily routine can strengthen your bond, reduce stress, and create a sense of emotional safety and comfort. Whether it's through morning cuddles, holding hands, or engaging in partner activities, these acts of physical closeness build a strong foundation for a loving and resilient relationship. So, go ahead and add a little more touch to your day—you'll feel the difference in your connection.

5.4 Emotional Bonding Exercises: Deepening the Connection

Let's face it: life can get pretty hectic. Between work, errands, and the occasional Netflix binge, it's easy to lose sight of the emotional connection that brought you and your partner together in the first place. That's where emotional bonding exercises come into play. These activities are designed to foster deeper emotional connections and understanding between partners. Think of them as relationship workouts—activities that strengthen the emotional muscles that keep your relationship thriving. Emotional intimacy is crucial in any marriage, as it creates a strong foundation of trust and mutual respect. When you feel emotionally connected to your partner, you're more likely to communicate openly, resolve conflicts effectively, and simply enjoy each other's company.

Sharing personal stories and memories is one of the simplest yet most effective emotional bonding exercises. Taking time to reminisce about your first date, a memorable vacation, or even a funny mishap can rekindle feelings of warmth and closeness. These stories serve as reminders of the bond you share and the experiences that have shaped your relationship. For instance, you might find yourselves laughing about the time you got lost on a road trip, turning what could have been a stressful situation into a cherished memory. Sharing these moments allows you to relive the emotions tied to them, reinforcing your connection.

Another powerful exercise involves asking and answering thought-provoking questions. These questions go beyond the surface, encouraging vulnerability and open communication. They can range from "What are your biggest dreams?" to "What do you think is the greatest strength of our relationship?" One popular activity is the "36 Questions that Lead to Love" exercise, where couples take turns answering a series of intimate questions designed to deepen their connection. This exercise encourages both partners to open up about their thoughts, fears, and aspirations, fostering a more profound understanding of each other.

Regular emotional bonding activities offer numerous benefits, enhancing intimacy and connection within the relationship. They encourage vulnerability, allowing both partners to share their innermost thoughts and feelings without fear of judgment. This openness strengthens the emotional foundation of the relationship, making it more resilient to challenges. When you engage in these activities regularly, you create a safe space for each other to be your true selves, free from the masks we often wear in our daily lives.

Real-life examples illustrate the transformative power of these exercises. Take Sarah and Mark, a couple who felt emotionally distant after years of marriage. They decided to dedicate time each week to sharing personal stories and answering thought-provoking questions. Over time, they found that these sessions brought them closer, reigniting the spark that had dimmed over the years. They discovered new things about each other and felt more connected than ever before. Another couple, Emily and Tom, overcame emotional distance by engaging in daily bonding activities like morning gratitude rituals and evening reflection sessions. These simple practices helped them build a stronger emotional connection, making their relationship more fulfilling and harmonious.

Incorporating emotional bonding exercises into your routine doesn't have to be complicated. Start with small, manageable activities and gradually build from there. For example, you could set aside 10 minutes each night to ask each other a thought-provoking question. Or, dedicate one evening a week to sharing personal stories and memories. The key is to make these activities a regular part of your relationship, ensuring you consistently nurture your emotional connection.

Focusing on emotional bonding exercises can deepen your connection with your partner, fostering a relationship built on trust, understanding, and mutual respect. These activities encourage vulnerability, open communication, and a more profound understanding of each other, creating a strong emotional foundation that supports a thriving marriage. So, grab those questions, share those stories, and watch your relationship flourish.

In this chapter, we've explored the importance of intimacy in its various forms, from weekly date nights to understanding love languages and enhancing physical and emotional connections. Each aspect plays a crucial role in building and maintaining a strong, healthy relationship. Okay, as we move forward, let's examine the practical tools and strategies to help you navigate common challenges and strengthen your partnership even further.

5.5 Feelings, Yuk! When Your Partner Can't Participate

I've been considering where to address an important part of this equation. What if your partner does not want to do 'touchy-feely' stuff? It's not that they don't love you or that they think there is nothing wrong with the relationship. It's just that they can't open up and be vulnerable. Engaging your partner to show and share their feelings can be a delicate process, as it often involves overcoming personal, cultural, or societal barriers to emotional expression. You have to be ready for this situation because it may be the first pushback you'll get. I got: 'I'm not doing that hippie stuff.' That first try ended up in an argument; I'm proud to say it didn't send me packing and running out the door. From subsequent attempts, I managed to get him to couples therapy. What was I thinking? He won't let himself be vulnerable in front of me; what made me think he would do it in front of a stranger? Silly me. Needless to say, that didn't last.

I've read so many boring books that I now find it difficult to pick one up. Many said the same things, and others advised flat-out manipulation, which I was not at all comfortable with. Thanks to the powers that be, he was open to short conversations. Slowly, I started to explain that aspects of our relationship needed a little TLC. This is where I get my cynicism about all things marriage. Love does NOT conquer all. You have to work on it repeatedly. You have to be patient; You have to put your money where your mouth is and show him how mindfulness and other techniques have helped you deal with HIM! Or you can leave. Don't make empty threats. Have a plan, and don't dangle leaving as if it were a carrot because leaving is not the point. Forging a kick-ass partnership is. I know you have to cut your losses at some point, but I want to know for certain that I tried everything.

Chapter 6:
Balancing Individual and Relationship Needs

Have you ever glanced at your calendar and realized you've scheduled an important meeting right on top of your partner's big work presentation? Or maybe you've finally found time for your favorite hobby, only to remember you promised to help your partner with a project? Balancing individual needs with relationship commitments can feel like juggling flaming torches while riding a unicycle. But fear not because this chapter is all about finding that elusive balance—where you can chase your dreams while still being the supportive partner you aspire to be.

6.1 Goal-Setting Workshops: Aligning Personal and Shared Objectives

Imagine you and your partner as co-pilots navigating life's turbulent skies. Without a clear destination and flight plan, you might end up circling aimlessly or crash-landing into conflict. That's where goal-setting comes in. Setting goals, both personal and shared is crucial for a healthy relationship. It's like having a roadmap that enhances mutual understanding and collaboration. When you both know where you're headed, supporting each other's journey is easier.

Goal-setting provides a roadmap for future growth and development. Whether planning a dream vacation, buying a house, or pursuing personal hobbies, having shared objectives ensures that you work towards common goals. This process not only fosters mutual understanding but also strengthens the sense of partnership. It's about creating a vision of your future together while respecting each other's aspirations. By aligning your goals, you reduce conflicts arising from divergent ambitions, creating a more harmonious relationship.

So, how do you set and align your goals effectively? Start by identifying individual aspirations and shared objectives. Have an open conversation where you both share your personal goals and discuss how they align with your relationship goals. This step ensures that both partners feel heard and valued. Next, create a vision board together. Grab some magazines, scissors, glue, and a poster board. Cut out images and words representing shared goals and dreams, both as individuals and as a couple. This visual representation constantly reminds you of what you're working towards. For example, if you both dream of traveling the world, include pictures of your desired destinations. If one partner aims to start a business while the other plans for further education, these ambitions are represented visually. This exercise makes goal-setting fun and deepens your connection as you visualize your future together.

Aligning personal and shared goals promotes a sense of teamwork and partnership. When both partners are on the same page, supporting each other's endeavors is easier. This alignment reduces conflicts arising from divergent goals, as you're both working towards a common vision. For instance, if one partner's goal is to advance their career, the other can provide support by taking on more household responsibilities. This mutual support fosters a sense of unity and strengthens the relationship. It's like paddling in the same direction in a tandem kayak—when both partners are in sync, you move forward smoothly.

To make goal-setting even more effective, use tools and resources that help articulate and plan your goals. Goal-setting worksheets can be incredibly helpful. Divide your goals into categories like career, health, and relationship. Write down your individual and shared goals for each category. This structured approach ensures that you cover all aspects of your life and relationship. Regular check-ins are also essential. Schedule monthly goal review sessions where you discuss your progress and any obstacles you face. This practice helps you stay on track and make necessary adjustments. For example, if you notice that a goal is taking longer to achieve than anticipated, you can brainstorm new strategies together. This continuous assessment and adjustment keep your goals relevant and achievable.

Exercise: Creating a Vision Board

33. Gather Materials: Collect magazines, scissors, glue, and a poster board.

34. Visualize Your Goals: Cut out images and words that represent your individual and shared goals.

35. Create Together: Arrange and glue the images on the poster board, visually representing your future.

36. Display Prominently: Place the vision board where you can see it daily as a reminder of your shared aspirations.

If you can't get them to cut and paste with you, have them show you an old catalog and have them describe what they want the future to be. Show them the finished product and see if they agree. They might even volunteer some suggestions at this point.

Goal-setting workshops are an effective way to align personal and shared objectives, enhancing mutual understanding and collaboration. By identifying individual aspirations, creating a vision board, and using goal-setting worksheets, you can create a roadmap for future growth and development. This process promotes teamwork, reduces conflicts, and strengthens your relationship. So, grab those magazines and start dreaming together!

6.2 Time Management for Couples: Maximizing Quality Time

Picture this: you're trying to juggle work deadlines, gym sessions, social events, and quality time with your partner. It's like trying to keep a dozen plates spinning without letting any crash to the ground. Effective time management in marriage is crucial because it ensures that quality time is prioritized despite busy schedules. When you manage your time well, you're less stressed and more balanced, making you a better partner. Think of it as clearing the clutter from your schedule so you can focus on what really matters—each other.

Managing time well in a relationship enhances satisfaction because it ensures you're carving out moments to connect, even amid chaos. A shared calendar can be a lifesaver here. Use it to schedule date nights, family time, and personal activities. This way, you both know what's coming up and can plan accordingly. For instance, if you know you have a big work project due, you can plan a relaxing evening together afterward as a reward. Time-blocking is another effective strategy. Dedicate specific blocks of time to different activities, including couple time. Setting aside dedicated time for each other ensures your relationship gets the attention it deserves.

Prioritization is critical when it comes to time management. Identify and focus on high-priority activities that align with your values and goals. This means saying no to things that don't contribute to your overall well-being or relationship. For example, if your partner values quality time but you're constantly working late, it might be time to reassess your priorities. Setting boundaries is also crucial. Protect your couple time by setting rules, like no work emails after 8 PM or no phones during dinner. These boundaries create a safe space where you can connect without distractions.

Weekly planning sessions can help you coordinate schedules and ensure you're both on the same page. Sit down together at the start of each week and review your upcoming commitments. Identify time slots for quality time and make adjustments as needed. This practice helps you stay organized and fosters communication and collaboration. For example, if you notice that you're both swamped with work, you can plan a low-key evening at home to unwind together. Time-tracking exercises can also be beneficial. Track how you spend your time for a week to identify any time-wasting activities. This awareness allows you to make more intentional choices about how you allocate your time.

Exercise: Weekly Planning Session

37. Set a Regular Time: Choose a consistent time each week for your planning session each week.

38. Review Schedules: Go over your individual and joint commitments.

39. Identify Quality Time: Find time slots for a couple of activities.

40. Make Adjustments: Adjust your schedules to ensure balance and prioritize each other.

Time management isn't just about squeezing more into your day; it's about making space for what truly matters. You can reduce stress, foster a balanced life, and enhance relationship satisfaction by managing your time effectively. So, grab that shared calendar, set your priorities straight, and start maximizing your quality time together.

6.3 Joint Decision-Making: Ensuring Both Partners Feel Valued

Have you ever tried to decide what to watch on Netflix and ended up scrolling for so long that you just went to bed instead? Now, imagine that scenario but with life's bigger decisions—finances, living arrangements, or even having kids. Joint decision-making in marriage is crucial because it ensures both partners feel valued and heard. It's not just about making choices together; it's about fostering a sense of equality and collaboration.

When both partners actively engage in decision-making, it promotes a healthy partnership where no one feels sidelined. You're both captains steering the ship; that shared responsibility can bring you closer. Discussing options openly and honestly is the first step. Lay out all the cards on the table and talk through each one. Maybe you're debating whether to move to a new city. One of you is excited about the job opportunities, while the other worries about leaving family behind. Weigh the pros and cons together. Create a list, and openly discuss your preferences. This way, you're not just focusing on what you want but understanding each other's perspectives.

Reaching a consensus or compromise is often where the magic happens. It's not about winning or losing; it's about finding a middle ground that works for both of you. Suppose you can't agree on whether to save for a house or take a big vacation. Maybe the compromise is setting aside some money for a smaller trip while still contributing to a house fund. This way, both partners feel their needs and desires are considered. A decision-making framework where you list the pros and cons of each option and discuss them openly can be a game-changer. It ensures transparency and mutual respect, making the process smoother.

However, joint decision-making isn't always a walk in the park. Differing opinions can create tension, and finding common ground can be challenging. One partner might be more dominant, leading to feelings of submission or resentment in the other. To overcome these obstacles, it's crucial to establish a balanced approach. Ensure that both voices are heard and valued. If one partner tends to dominate, gently remind them of the importance of equal input. On the flip side, if one partner tends to shy away from making decisions, encourage them to share their thoughts and feelings. It's about creating a safe space where both partners feel comfortable expressing their views.

Practicing joint decision-making can improve these skills over time. Role-playing scenarios where joint decisions are required can be incredibly helpful. Imagine you're making a financial investment. One partner plays the role of the cautious investor, while the other is more adventurous. Practice discussing options, weighing pros and cons, and reaching a consensus. This exercise helps you understand each other's decision-making styles and find ways to collaborate effectively.

Keeping a "decision diary" can also be beneficial. Document and reflect on your decision-making process. Record the decisions you've made, the steps you took, and any lessons learned. For example, if you decided to adopt a pet, jot down the discussions you had, the compromises made, and how you reached the final decision. Reviewing this diary can provide valuable insights into your collaborative process, helping you refine and improve it over time.

Joint decision-making is essential for a healthy partnership because it ensures both partners feel valued and heard. You can foster a sense of equality and collaboration by discussing options openly, weighing pros and cons, and reaching a consensus or compromise. Overcoming challenges like differing opinions and dominance requires a balanced approach and open communication. Practicing joint decision-making through role-playing scenarios and maintaining a decision diary can further enhance your collaborative skills. So, the next time you face a big decision, remember that you're in this together and together, you can navigate anything.

6.4 Supporting Each Other's Dreams: Encouragement and Compromise

Imagine this: your partner comes home, all fired up about a new business idea, or maybe they've decided to train for a marathon. Supporting each other's dreams is crucial for a thriving relationship. It promotes individual growth and fulfillment, which translates into a happier and more balanced partnership. When you encourage your partner to pursue their aspirations, you're not just helping them achieve personal success; you're also strengthening the bond and trust between you. It's like watering a plant—both the individual and the relationship flourish.

So, how do you offer this support in a meaningful way? Start by actively listening and showing genuine interest in each other's goals. When your partner talks about their dreams, put down your phone, make eye contact, and really listen. Ask questions, show enthusiasm, and tell them you're excited about their aspirations. For example, if your partner is preparing for a job interview, help them practice their responses, give feedback, or even help them pick out the perfect outfit. This kind of practical help and resource-sharing demonstrates that you're invested in their success.

Offering practical help and resources is another way to show support. If your partner wants to start a new hobby, like painting, consider buying them a set of quality paints or signing them up for a class. If they're aiming for a promotion, help them update their resume or connect them with people in your network who can offer advice. These tangible acts of support make it easier for your partner to pursue their goals and show that you're willing to go the extra mile for their happiness.

Compromise plays a significant role in supporting each other's dreams, especially when individual aspirations might conflict with relationship commitments. Finding a balance between personal and shared goals is essential. It's about negotiating and making trade-offs to ensure both partners feel valued. For instance, if one partner wants to return to school while the other is focused on saving for a house, you'll need to find a middle ground. Maybe you agree to budget more strictly or take on extra work to make both dreams possible. This balance ensures that neither partner feels like they're sacrificing too much for the other.

Practicing support and compromise can be enhanced through specific activities. "Dream sharing" sessions are a great way to start. Set aside time to discuss your individual and shared aspirations. Take turns talking about what you want to achieve and brainstorm ways to support each other. For example, if your partner dreams of starting a side business, discuss how you can help, whether by taking on more household responsibilities or offering moral support during busy times. These sessions foster understanding and create a plan for mutual support.

Compromise exercises can help you practice finding solutions that work for both partners. Choose a scenario where individual aspirations might conflict and role-play how you would negotiate and make trade-offs. For instance, if one partner wants to spend weekends working on a personal project while the other wants to spend time together, discuss how you can balance both needs. Maybe you agree to dedicate certain weekends to the project and others to quality time together. Practicing these scenarios helps you develop the skills needed to navigate real-life conflicts effectively.

Supporting each other's dreams creates an environment where both partners feel encouraged and valued. By actively listening, offering practical help, and practicing compromise, you can promote individual growth while strengthening your bond. Dream-sharing sessions and compromise exercises provide helpful ways to enhance your support and negotiation skills. So, the next time your partner shares their aspirations, remember that your encouragement and willingness to compromise can make all the difference.

6.5 Self-Care in Marriage: Taking Care of You to Take Care of Us

Ever felt like you're running on fumes, trying to juggle work, family, and social life, only to realize you haven't taken a moment for yourself in weeks? Welcome to the club. Self-care isn't just a buzzword; it's crucial for your well-being and the health of your marriage. When you take care of yourself, you're promoting your happiness and enhancing your ability to be a supportive and present partner. Think of self-care as the fuel that keeps your relationship's engine running smoothly. Without it, you're likely to stall.

Establishing a self-care routine is a great place to start. It doesn't have to be elaborate. Maybe it's a morning run, a weekly yoga class, or even just 15 minutes of reading before bed. The key is consistency. Set boundaries to protect your personal time and energy. If you're constantly saying yes to everyone else, you'll end up with nothing left for yourself or your partner. Create a self-care checklist with daily, weekly, and monthly activities. This could include anything from taking a relaxing bath to attending a monthly book club. By scheduling these activities, you ensure that self-care becomes a regular part of your life.

The role of mutual support in self-care can't be overstated. Encourage and respect each other's self-care routines. If your partner needs time to unwind with a hobby, support them by taking on extra responsibilities during that time. Participating in self-care activities together can also be incredibly bonding. Couples' yoga, for instance, promotes physical well-being and fosters emotional connection. Imagine both of you stretching, breathing, and laughing together—it's a great way to relax and reconnect. Mutual support ensures that both partners feel valued and understood, creating a more harmonious relationship.

Integrating self-care into your relationship can be both fun and effective. Start with "self-care planning" sessions, where you discuss and plan your individual and joint self-care activities. Sit down with your partner and create a schedule that includes personal and shared self-care time. For example, you might decide Sunday mornings are for solo activities like reading or jogging. Saturday evenings are for joint activities like a movie night or a couples' massage. These planning sessions help you both prioritize self-care and ensure it becomes a regular part of your routine.

Accountability exercises can also be beneficial. Check-in on each other's self-care progress. Ask questions like, "Did you get a chance to do your yoga this week?" or "How was your time at the book club?" These check-ins show that you care about each other's well-being and help keep self-care on the agenda. For instance, if your partner has been neglecting their self-care routine, a gentle reminder from you can encourage them to get back on track. Accountability fosters a supportive environment where both partners feel motivated to care for themselves.

Exercise: Self-Care Planning Session

41. Schedule a Time: Set aside an hour for a self-care planning session.

42. Discuss Routines: Talk about your current self-care activities and what you'd like to add.

43. Create a Schedule: Plan daily, weekly, and monthly self-care activities for both personal and joint time.

44. Check-In Regularly: Set a time for weekly check-ins to discuss your progress and make adjustments as needed.

Taking care of yourself is not a luxury; it's a necessity for a healthy, happy relationship. Establishing a self-care routine, setting boundaries, and supporting each other's efforts can create an environment where both partners thrive. Self-care planning sessions and accountability exercises provide practical ways to integrate self-care into your relationship, ensuring it becomes a regular and valued part of your life together.

Balancing individual and relationship needs is like walking a tightrope, but with the right tools, you can find that sweet spot where both you and your partner feel fulfilled. Whether setting goals, managing time, making decisions together, supporting each other's dreams, or prioritizing self-care, each aspect contributes to a stronger, more resilient relationship. As you continue to navigate these challenges, remember that it's all about working together and supporting each other every step of the way.

Next, we'll dive into overcoming jealousy and insecurity, exploring strategies to strengthen trust and build a more secure relationship. Stay tuned for more insights and practical advice.

Chapter 7:
Overcoming Jealousy and Insecurity

Imagine this: You're scrolling through Instagram, and you see a picture of your partner at a party, laughing with someone you don't know. Suddenly, your heart races, your palms get sweaty, and a little green monster starts whispering in your ear. We've all been there. Jealousy can sneak up on you like that unexpected final exam you forgot to study for. But here's the thing—it's not just about that one Instagram post. To really tackle jealousy, you need to get to the root of it. Let's dig in.

7.1 Identifying Triggers: Understanding the Root Causes

Understanding the root causes of jealousy is like finding the source of a mysterious leak in your house. You can mop up the water all you want, but until you fix the leak, the problem will keep coming back. Identifying what triggers your jealousy helps you recognize patterns and pinpoint situations that provoke these feelings. This is crucial because it provides a starting point for addressing the underlying issues. Jealousy isn't just a random emotion that pops up from nowhere; it's usually tied to something more profound.

Common triggers for jealousy can vary widely but often revolve around past experiences and traumas. Maybe you've been cheated on before, and now every friendly interaction your partner has feels like a potential threat. Comparisons with others can also stir the pot. Ever find yourself comparing your relationship to your partner's ex or even your best friend's seemingly perfect love life? It's like trying to measure up to an Instagram filter—unrealistic and stressful. Fear of abandonment or loss is another major trigger. If you've experienced significant loss or instability in the past, you might be hyper-alert to any signs that your partner might leave you. For example, if your partner has a close friendship with a colleague, it might trigger fears of being replaced or not being enough.

Personal insecurities often play a starring role in the drama of jealousy. Low self-esteem and self-worth can magnify every little thing, turning molehills into mountains. It's easy to project those insecurities onto your relationship if you don't feel confident in yourself. The fear of not being enough for your partner can gnaw at you, making you question their every move and interaction. It's like having a little voice in your head constantly whispering, "You're not good enough," which can be exhausting and damaging to you and your relationship.

To tackle this beast head-on, it's essential to identify your personal triggers. One effective method is through journaling. Take some time each day to reflect on moments when you felt jealous. Write down what happened, how you felt, and what thoughts went through your mind. This exercise helps you spot patterns and understand what specifically triggers your jealousy. Maybe you notice that you feel jealous every time your partner mentions a particular friend. Understanding this can help you address the root cause. Another helpful tool is self-assessment quizzes. These quizzes can guide you in identifying patterns of insecurity. They often include questions like, "Do you frequently compare yourself to others?" or "Do you fear that your partner will leave you?" Answering these questions honestly can provide insights into your triggers.

Exercise: Journaling to Identify Jealousy Triggers

45. Set Aside Time: Dedicate 10-15 minutes each day for journaling.

46. Document Jealousy Instances: Write down any moments when you felt jealous. Include details like what happened, how you felt, and any thoughts that crossed your mind.

47. Analyze Triggers: After documenting for a week, review your entries to identify common triggers and patterns.

For example, you might write, "Today, I felt jealous when I saw my partner chatting with their colleague. It made me feel like I'm not good enough, and I fear they might prefer spending time with their colleague over me." This reflection can help you understand that your jealousy may stem from personal insecurities rather than your partner's actions.

Identifying the root causes of jealousy is the first step towards addressing it. By recognizing patterns and pinpointing specific triggers, you can start to understand what's driving these feelings. It's like turning on the lights in a dark room—you can finally see what you're dealing with. Whether it's past traumas, comparisons, or personal insecurities, understanding these triggers provides a foundation for addressing and overcoming jealousy. So grab that journal, take those quizzes, and start digging deep. You've got this!

7.2 Open Conversations: Discussing Jealousy Constructively

Envision you're sitting on the couch, and your partner mentions how much fun they had at lunch with a colleague. Suddenly, a wave of jealousy hits you, but instead of stewing silently, you decide to talk about it. Here's the thing—open communication about jealousy is crucial. It promotes understanding and empathy between you and your partner, preventing misunderstandings and resentment from building up. When you keep these feelings bottled up, they fester and eventually explode, often leading to bigger conflicts.

Discussing jealousy openly isn't about pointing fingers; it's about expressing your feelings in a way that fosters dialogue rather than defensiveness. Start with "I" statements to articulate your emotions without blaming your partner. For example, instead of saying, "You always spend too much time with your friend," try, "I feel insecure when you spend a lot of time with your friend because I worry about our connection." This phrasing focuses on your feelings and concerns, making it easier for your partner to understand your perspective without feeling attacked. Choosing the right time and setting for these conversations is also important. Bringing it up in the middle of a heated argument or when either of you is distracted isn't going to help. Find a calm, private moment when you can both focus on the discussion.

Active listening plays a critical role in these conversations. It's not enough to talk about your feelings; you must listen to each other's perspectives. Reflect back what your partner says to ensure you understand their point of view. For instance, if they say, "I didn't realize spending time with my friend made you feel this way," you might respond, "So, you didn't see it from my perspective and didn't intend to make me feel insecure." This reflection shows you're engaged and trying to understand their side, which can help validate each other's feelings and experiences. Validating your partner's feelings doesn't mean you have to agree with them. It's about acknowledging their emotions and showing empathy.

Now, let's consider some practical activities to help you practice discussing jealousy constructively. Role-playing conversations about jealousy can be incredibly useful. Choose a common scenario that triggers jealousy and take turns expressing your feelings. For example, if you often feel jealous about your partner's friendship with a coworker, role-play a conversation where you express your feelings using "I" statements. Your partner can then practice active listening and reflecting back what they hear. This exercise helps both of you get comfortable with the process and reduces the likelihood of defensive reactions during honest conversations.

Another helpful tool is a "jealousy discussion" worksheet. This can guide your conversation and ensure you cover all the essential points. The worksheet might include prompts like, "What specific situation triggered your jealousy?" "How did it make you feel?" and "What can we do together to address this?" Filling out the worksheet together can help you structure the conversation and ensure both partners have a chance to share their thoughts and feelings. It also provides a written record you can refer to if the issue arises again.

Exercise: Role-Playing Jealousy Conversations

48. Choose a Scenario: Pick an ordinary situation that triggers jealousy in your relationship.

49. Express Feelings: Take turns expressing your feelings using "I" statements. For example, "I feel jealous when you spend time with your coworker because I worry about our connection."

50. Practice Active Listening: The listening partner should echo what they hear. For instance, "So, spending time with my coworker makes you feel insecure about our relationship?"

51. Switch Roles: Repeat the exercise with the roles reversed.

Open conversations about jealousy are essential for maintaining a healthy relationship. Discussing your feelings openly and constructively can promote understanding and empathy, preventing misunderstandings and resentment from building up. Key components of these conversations are using "I" statements, choosing the right time and setting, and practicing active listening. Role-playing and discussion worksheets can help you practice and refine these skills, making it easier to handle jealousy constructively in your relationship.

7.3 Building Self-Worth: Confidence in Relationships

Alright, let's talk about self-worth. Imagine you're at a party and you see someone who radiates confidence. They walk with their head held high, smile easily, and seem at ease in their own skin. That's the kind of self-worth we're aiming for, and it's a game-changer when it comes to overcoming jealousy. Building self-confidence helps reduce feelings of jealousy because it enhances your personal security and reduces your dependence on external validation. When you feel good about yourself, you're less likely to feel threatened by others. This shift promotes a healthier, more balanced relationship where both partners feel secure and valued.

So, how do you build self-worth? It starts with positive affirmations and self-compassion practices. Think of it as giving yourself a little pep talk each day. Try this: create a list of personal strengths and achievements to review daily. It's like having a mini cheerleading squad in your pocket, reminding you how awesome you are. For instance, write down things like, "I am a great listener," or "I handled that work project like a pro." Reviewing these daily affirmations can boost your confidence and help you focus on your positive qualities rather than dwelling on insecurities. Pursuing personal interests and hobbies is another excellent way to build self-worth. When you engage in activities that you love and excel at, it reinforces your sense of competence and satisfaction. Whether painting, hiking, or playing an instrument, doing something you're passionate about can significantly boost your self-esteem.

Personal growth plays a crucial role in relationship dynamics. When both partners are committed to their individual development, it creates a more dynamic and fulfilling relationship. Encouraging mutual growth and self-improvement means supporting each other's personal goals and aspirations. For example, if your partner wants to take a night class to learn a new skill, cheer them on and maybe even help them study. This mutual support fosters a sense of partnership and helps both of you grow individually and together. It's like planting seeds in a garden—you nurture each other's growth, and in turn, your relationship blossoms.

To practice building self-worth, try keeping an "affirmation journal." Each day, write down positive affirmations about yourself. These could be simple statements like, "I am worthy of love and respect" or "I am capable and strong." This daily practice helps reinforce positive self-beliefs and gradually shifts your mindset. Another helpful exercise is self-reflection. Take time to identify and challenge negative self-beliefs. Write down your negative thoughts about yourself and then counter them with positive affirmations. For example, if you think, "I'm not good enough," counter it with, "I am more than enough just as I am." This exercise helps you recognize and replace negative thought patterns with positive ones.

Exercise: Affirmation Journal

52. Start a Journal: Get a notebook dedicated to your affirmations.

53. Daily Affirmations: Write down positive affirmations about yourself each day, such as "I am worthy of love and respect" or "I am capable and strong."

54. Reflect and Review: Take a few minutes each evening to review your affirmations and reflect on how they made you feel.

Building self-worth takes time and effort, but the rewards are immense. When you feel confident and secure in yourself, it transforms your relationship. You're less likely to feel threatened by external factors and more likely to support and celebrate each other's growth. So, grab that journal, start listing your strengths, and watch your confidence soar.

7.4 Reassurance Techniques: Strengthening Trust and Security

Imagine you're building a house. The foundation is solid, and the walls are up, but without regular maintenance, even the sturdiest house can start to crumble. That's where reassurance comes in. Providingpships, providing and seeking reassurance is crucial for overcoming jealousy and insecurity. It reinforces trust and safety between partners, helping to calm those lurking fears and anxieties that can gnaw away at your connection. When your partner feels reassured, they know you're committed, which helps to stabilize the relationship, making it more resilient against the waves of doubt and jealousy.

So, how do you actually go about providing reassurance? Start with verbal affirmations of love and commitment. Regularly telling your partner, "I love you and am committed to our relationship," can work wonders. It might sound simple, but those words carry a lot of weight. They serve as constant reminders that you're in this together, come what may. Consistent and reliable behavior also goes a long way. Demonstrating that you can be depended on reinforces your partner's sense of security. For instance, always showing up when you say you will and following through on promises builds a solid track record of reliability. This consistency helps to cement trust, making it easier for your partner to feel secure in the relationship.

Consistency is an integral part when it comes to providing reassurance. Keeping promises and following through on commitments shows you're dependable and predictable. It's like having a reliable Wi-Fi connection—you don't have to worry about dropping out when you need it most. When your actions consistently align with your words, it builds a strong foundation of trust. Being dependable means that your partner knows they can count on you, which helps to alleviate fears and anxieties. While it might sound boring, predictable behavior creates a safe and stable environment where trust can flourish.

Incorporating reassurance into your daily interactions doesn't have to be a chore. Think of it as adding little love notes to your relationship. Reassurance rituals, like daily affirmations or check-ins, can become cherished parts of your routine. Imagine starting each day by telling your partner one thing you appreciate about them. It could be as simple as "I love how you always make me laugh." These small acts of affirmation add up, creating a reservoir of positive feelings to draw from when times get tough. Trust-building activities are another great way to reinforce reassurance. Practice consistent and reliable actions, like setting aside time each week to discuss your relationship and any concerns you might have. This regular check-in helps to address issues before they become serious problems, reinforcing your commitment to each other.

Exercise: Daily Reassurance Ritual

55. Set a Time: Choose a specific time each day for your reassurance ritual, such as during breakfast or before bed.

56. Express Love and Commitment: Take turns expressing your love and commitment to each other. For example, "I love you and am grateful for how you support me."

57. Reflect and Appreciate: Reflect on the day and share one thing you appreciate about your partner. This could be something they did or a quality you admire.

This daily reassurance ritual helps to build a habit of expressing love and commitment, reinforcing the security of your relationship.

Reassurance is the glue that holds the fabric of trust together. By consistently providing and seeking reassurance, you create a stable and secure environment where jealousy and insecurity have less room to grow. You reinforce your commitment to each other through verbal affirmations, dependable behavior, and regular trust-building activities, making your relationship more resilient and fulfilling. So, start incorporating these small yet powerful actions into your daily routine and watch your relationship flourish with a renewed sense of trust and security.

7.5 Real-Life Strategies: Couples Who Conquered Jealousy

Jealousy can feel like a dark cloud hanging over a relationship, but let me tell you, there are couples who have managed to clear the skies. Take Jenna and Mike, for example. They found themselves constantly bickering over Jenna's friendship with a male colleague. The jealousy was eating away at their relationship until they decided to face it head-on. They started by scheduling weekly check-ins where they could openly discuss their feelings without judgment. During these check-ins, they practiced active listening and made sure to validate each other's emotions. Jenna would say, "I understand this makes you uncomfortable, and I'm here to reassure you," Mike would respond with, "I appreciate your reassurance; it helps me feel more secure." Over time, these open conversations helped them build a stronger foundation of trust and understanding.

Another couple, Sarah and Tom, battled jealousy that stemmed from Sarah's low self-esteem. Sarah often felt threatened by Tom's close friendships, interpreting them as signs that she wasn't enough. They decided to tackle the issue by focusing on building Sarah's self-worth. Sarah started journaling daily affirmations and took up painting, a hobby she loved but had neglected. Tom supported her by attending her art shows and celebrating her progress. They also sought professional help through couples therapy, where they learned techniques to support each other's growth and address their insecurities. The combination of personal development and mutual support helped Sarah feel more confident, which in turn reduced her jealousy.

The emotional journey of overcoming jealousy is not a walk in the park. It starts with an initial struggle and pain that can feel overwhelming. Jenna and Mike had their fair share of late-night arguments and tears. Sarah often felt inadequate and questioned her worth. But the key is to stick with it. Gradually, as trust and security build, those intense feelings of jealousy start to diminish. It's like climbing a mountain; the first few steps are the hardest, but each step gets you closer to the summit. For Jenna and Mike, the weekly check-ins became less about jealousy and more about sharing their lives. For Sarah and Tom, therapy sessions turned from addressing insecurities to celebrating growth.

Encouraging quotes from these couples can offer a beacon of hope. Jenna says, "We learned that trust is built one day at a time, and it's worth the effort." Tom adds, "Seeing Sarah grow into her confidence was the best thing for both of us. It's amazing how much stronger we are now." Their stories show that overcoming jealousy is possible with dedication and effort.

Practical advice from these couples can guide you on your path. Jenna and Mike recommend setting aside dedicated time for check-ins, with no phones or distractions—just honest conversation. Sarah and Tom advocate for personal growth. "Find something you're passionate about and immerse yourself in it," Sarah advises. "It's not just about feeling better about yourself; it's about growing as a person, which positively impacts your relationship."

Here's another example. Emma and Jake struggled with jealousy when Emma started a new job that required a lot of travel. Jake felt insecure about Emma being away and meeting new people. They implemented daily reassurance rituals like morning texts and evening video calls to stay connected. They also engaged in trust-building activities, such as planning surprise visits and sharing their schedules to maintain transparency. These actions helped Jake feel more secure, and Emma appreciated the effort to keep their connection strong, even when apart.

The emotional journey of overcoming jealousy is filled with ups and downs, but the triumphs make it worthwhile. It's about moving from a place of fear and insecurity to one of trust and confidence. The key is to keep pushing forward, even when it feels tough. The initial struggle is real, but so is the reward. Couples like Jenna and Mike, Sarah and Tom, and Emma and Jake show that overcoming jealousy is not just a dream but a reachable reality with perseverance, open communication, and mutual support. So, take heart and start your journey today.

And with that, we wrap up our exploration of overcoming jealousy and insecurity. Next, we'll dive into redefining marriage in the 21st century, exploring how modern values and societal shifts are reshaping this timeless institution. Stay tuned.

Chapter 8:
Redefining Marriage in the 21st Century

Have you ever tried explaining your relationship to your grandma and watched her eyes glaze over? You say "polyamory," and she thinks you're talking about a new type of plant. Times have changed, and so have relationships. Welcome to the 21st century, where marriage doesn't fit neatly into the old box anymore. Let's dive into the fascinating world of non-traditional relationship models and see what's beyond the white picket fence.

8.1 Diverse Relationships: Beyond Traditional Norms

Let's kick things off with polyamory and open relationships. Picture this: instead of the classic one-on-one relationship, you have multiple romantic partners. It's like having a romantic buffet instead of a single entrée. Polyamory involves having consensual, loving relationships with more than one person. Everyone knows about everyone else, and communication is vital. It's not just about physical connections—emotional bonds play a significant role too. Open relationships, on the other hand, usually involve a primary couple who agree that it's okay to have sexual relationships with other people. The main difference? Open relationships might not have the same emotional depth with secondary partners as polyamory does.

Then, there's the concept of co-living arrangements and communal living. Think of it as a modern twist on the old hippie communes. Co-living arrangements involve multiple people, often friends or like-minded individuals, sharing a living space and sometimes even resources. It's like an extended family without the awkward holiday dinners. Communal living takes it a step further, with a group of people sharing not just living space but also responsibilities, meals, and, often, a communal lifestyle philosophy. These setups can foster a strong sense of community and support but also require clear agreements and boundaries to avoid conflicts.

Long-distance marriages and commuter marriages are becoming increasingly common. With globalization and job opportunities scattered around the globe, it's not unusual for couples to live in different cities, states, or even countries. These relationships rely heavily on digital communication and regular visits to maintain the connection. It's like being in a relationship with your phone's calendar app— planning visits, video calls, and virtual date nights become essential. While the physical distance can be challenging, many couples find that the time apart makes their time together even more special.

Now, let's consider the benefits and challenges of these diverse relationships. One significant advantage is increased flexibility and personal freedom. In polyamorous relationships, for example, you have the freedom to explore different aspects of your personality with different partners. Maybe one partner loves hiking while the other is your go-to for deep philosophical debates. It's like having a Swiss Army knife of relationships, each partner bringing something unique to the table. However, this flexibility can also lead to potential jealousy and complex dynamics. Imagine juggling schedules and emotions with multiple partners—it can be like herding cats on a tightrope.

Co-living arrangements and communal living offer the benefit of shared resources and support. Imagine having multiple people to share chores, expenses, and emotional support. It's like having a built-in support system. However, with various people come multiple opinions and potential conflicts. Navigating these dynamics requires excellent communication and the ability to compromise. Long-distance marriages, while offering the freedom to pursue career opportunities in different locations, can strain emotional and physical intimacy. Maintaining a connection across miles takes effort, creativity, and a lot of trust.

Let's dive into some real-life examples. Meet the Johnsons, a polyamorous family managing multiple partnerships with grace and humor. They have a weekly "family meeting" where everyone gets together to discuss schedules, feelings, and any issues that might arise. It's like a relationship board meeting, complete with snacks. Then there's Emily and Jake, a couple in a long-distance marriage. Emily works in New York, while Jake's job keeps him in San Francisco. They maintain their connection through nightly video calls, virtual date nights, and monthly visits. Their secret? A shared Google calendar and a lot of airline miles.

So, how does society view these non-traditional relationships? It's a mixed bag. Legal recognition and rights for diverse relationships vary widely. Some countries and states are more progressive, offering legal protections and recognition, while others lag behind. Social support and stigma also play significant roles. While younger generations tend to be more accepting, older generations might struggle understanding these relationship dynamics. Take the case of the Smiths, a polyamorous family navigating legal challenges and societal perceptions. They've faced everything from curious questions to outright judgment but have found a supportive community that embraces their lifestyle.

Navigating these diverse relationships requires a mix of patience, open communication, and a willingness to challenge traditional norms. Whether you're in a polyamorous relationship, a co-living arrangement, or a long-distance marriage, the key is to find what works best for you and your partners. It's all about creating a relationship dynamic that feels authentic and fulfilling. So, go ahead and redefine what marriage means for you. The 21st century is all about breaking the mold and creating new, exciting ways to connect.

8.2 Inclusivity in Marriage: Embracing All Forms of Love

Inclusivity in marriage is all about embracing and celebrating diversity in every form. It means recognizing and validating love and partnerships across the spectrum of sexual orientations, gender identities, and cultural backgrounds. Imagine a world where love isn't confined by traditional norms, where your choice of partner doesn't invite judgment or scorn. That's the essence of inclusivity. It's about understanding that love is love, whether between two men, two women, a man and a woman, or any other combination. It also means respecting and honoring the unique cultural rituals and traditions that couples bring into their relationships.

Inclusivity is more than just a buzzword; it's a cornerstone of a healthy society. We promote equality and human rights when we embrace diverse forms of love. This means everyone has the right to love who they love without fear of discrimination or prejudice. Inclusive marriages contribute to a more compassionate and understanding society by breaking down barriers and challenging outdated norms. Reducing discrimination isn't just about changing laws; it's about changing hearts and minds. When people see inclusive relationships thriving, holding on to prejudiced views becomes harder. It also fosters empathy and understanding, making society kinder and more accepting overall.

So, how do you foster inclusivity in your own marriage? Start by educating yourself about different identities and experiences. Read books, attend workshops, and seek out resources that broaden your understanding. For instance, attending workshops on LGBTQ+ issues can provide valuable insights into the challenges faced by these communities and how you can offer support. Practicing empathy and open-mindedness is also crucial. Put yourself in your partner's shoes, especially if they come from a different background or identify differently than you. This means listening without judgment and being willing to learn and grow together.

Take, for example, the story of Mark and James, a same-sex couple who navigated societal challenges to build a life together. They faced everything from casual discrimination to outright hostility, but their commitment to each other and their willingness to educate those around them made a significant difference. They attended local LGBTQ+ support groups and even spoke at community events to raise awareness. Their openness and bravery not only strengthened their bond but also helped foster a more inclusive environment in their community.

Another inspiring example is Maria and David, a mixed-race couple who celebrate their cultural diversity. They enriched their relationship and honor each other's traditions and backgrounds, from cooking traditional meals to celebrating cultural holidays. They've also educated their families about the importance of respecting their diverse heritage. For their wedding, they blended elements from both cultures, creating a ceremony that was uniquely theirs. This not only enriched their relationship but also brought their families closer together, fostering mutual respect and understanding.

Practical Exercise: Fostering Inclusivity in Your Relationship

58. Educate Yourself: Pick a book or attend a workshop on inclusivity-related topics, LGBTQ+ issues, or cultural diversity.

59. Practice Empathy: Spend time listening to your partner's experiences and perspectives, especially if they differ from your own.

60. Celebrate Diversity: Incorporate elements of each other's cultural or identity backgrounds into your daily life or special occasions.

Inclusivity in marriage isn't just about accepting differences; it's about celebrating them. You can create a more inclusive and loving partnership by educating yourself, practicing empathy, and actively incorporating diverse elements into your relationship. It's about building a relationship that not only withstands societal pressures but also stands as a beacon of love and acceptance in a world that desperately needs it. So, embrace the diversity in your relationship and let it enrich your lives in ways you never imagined possible.

8.3 Modern Challenges: Work-Life Balance and Gender Roles

Envision this: you're juggling a demanding career, a household, and maybe even kids. It's like performing a one-person circus act, complete with flaming hoops and high-wire acts. Modern work demands have turned our lives into a complex balancing act, affecting relationship dynamics in ways our grandparents could never have imagined. The stress of managing both career and family responsibilities can feel overwhelming. You're trying to finish a work project while helping your child with homework, and suddenly, you realize you haven't had a meaningful conversation with your partner in days.

Flexible work arrangements can be a lifesaver here. Remote work, flex hours, and job sharing can provide the breathing room needed to balance career ambitions with family life. Imagine a couple where both partners have demanding careers but manage to carve out quality family time thanks to flexible work schedules. They set boundaries, designating certain hours as "no work zones" to ensure they're fully present for their kids and each other. This balance helps them manage their time more effectively, reducing stress and improving their overall relationship satisfaction.

Gender roles are also evolving rapidly in modern marriages. Gone are the days when men were the sole breadwinners and women were confined to domestic duties. The rise of dual-income households has led to significant shifts in domestic responsibilities and caregiving roles. Today, you'll find dads changing diapers and moms leading board meetings. This shift has brought both opportunities and challenges. On the one hand, sharing responsibilities promotes equality and partnership. On the other hand, constant negotiation and balancing are required to ensure neither partner feels overwhelmed. Couples must communicate their expectations openly and be willing to adapt as circumstances change.

Achieving work-life balance isn't just about juggling tasks; it's about setting boundaries and prioritizing what matters most. One practical tip is to create a shared schedule to ensure both partners have time for work, family, and personal interests. This might mean blocking out time for date nights, family outings, and even solo activities that recharge your batteries. Prioritizing quality time and self-care is crucial. You can't pour from an empty cup; neglecting self-care can lead to burnout and resentment. Imagine a couple who sets aside Sunday afternoons for family hikes, ensuring they stay connected and active. They also schedule "me time" for each partner, allowing them to pursue personal hobbies and interests.

Real-life examples can provide valuable insights into navigating these challenges. Take Sarah and Tom, for instance. Both have demanding careers but use remote work to their advantage. They coordinate their schedules to maximize time together, often working side by side at home. They also prioritize family dinners and weekend trips to maintain their bond. Another example is Lisa and Mike, who have redefined their roles to support each other's careers. When Lisa decided to go back to school, Mike took on more household responsibilities to give her the space she needed to study. This mutual support strengthened their relationship, making them more resilient as a couple.

Navigating work-life balance and evolving gender roles requires a combination of flexibility, communication, and mutual support. Whether setting boundaries between work and home life, prioritizing quality time, or redefining traditional roles, the key is finding what works best for you and your partner. It's about creating a partnership where both of you feel valued, supported, and fulfilled. So, grab your calendar, set those boundaries, and make sure you get the time and space you need to thrive—both individually and together.

8.4 Digital Age Relationships: Navigating Social Media and Privacy

Ever felt like your relationship had an audience it didn't ask for? Modern marriages often come with an uninvited peanut gallery thanks to social media. Maintaining a public image on platforms like Instagram and Facebook can feel like walking a tightrope. You're posting pictures of your latest vacation or anniversary dinner, but behind the scenes, you might be dealing with stress or disagreements. The pressure to present a picture-perfect relationship can be overwhelming. It's easy to fall into the trap of comparing your real life to others' highlight reels, leading to feelings of inadequacy and envy. This constant need to showcase happiness can drive a wedge between partners, creating a façade that's hard to maintain.

Jealousy and misunderstandings can also rear their ugly heads in the digital age. Imagine your partner gets a friendly comment from an old friend, and suddenly, you're spiraling into a jealousy-fueled panic. Or perhaps you see photos of a night out that you knew nothing about, and now you're feeling left out and suspicious. Social media can amplify these feelings, making minor issues seem monumental. The lack of context in online interactions can lead to misinterpretations and conflicts that might not have arisen otherwise. It's like trying to read between the lines of a text message and coming up with a novel's worth of drama.

In this era of oversharing, maintaining privacy is crucial. Setting boundaries for social media usage can help protect your relationship from unnecessary scrutiny and drama. Decide together what aspects of your relationship you're comfortable sharing online and what should remain private. This could mean limiting posts about personal conflicts or avoiding oversharing intimate details. Trust and transparency play key roles in managing digital interactions. Openly discuss your online activities and concerns with each other to prevent misunderstandings. Consider the example of a couple who set ground rules for what they share about their relationship online. They agreed not to post about arguments or personal issues, focusing instead on positive, non-intrusive content.

Strategies for healthy digital communication are essential for navigating the online world without compromising your relationship. Regularly disconnecting from devices to focus on each other is a simple yet effective strategy. Set aside tech-free times, like during meals or before bed, to foster real-life connections. Communicating openly about online activities and concerns can also prevent issues from escalating. If something online bothers you, address it calmly and directly with your partner instead of letting it fester. This openness can build trust and ensure that both of you feel secure in your digital interactions.

Real-life examples can offer valuable insights into managing digital challenges. Take Sarah and John, for instance. They realized their constant social media use was creating distance between them. They decided to reduce their online presence and focus more on each other. They set specific times for social media use and committed to spending their evenings device-free. This change significantly improved their relationship, allowing them to reconnect and communicate more effectively. Another example is Lisa and Mark, who maintain trust and privacy despite being active online. They openly discuss their online interactions and respect each other's boundaries, ensuring that their digital lives don't interfere with their real-world connection.

Navigating social media and privacy in modern marriages requires a blend of communication, trust, and intentionality. By setting boundaries, prioritizing real-life interactions, and being transparent about online activities, you can protect your relationship from the pitfalls of the digital age. It's about finding a balance that allows you to enjoy the benefits of social media without letting it dictate the dynamics of your relationship. So, the next time you're tempted to post that perfect couple selfie, take a moment to check in with your partner first. After all, the best moments are often the ones that don't make it to Instagram.

8.5 The Future of Marriage: Trends and Predictions

Visualize this: you're at a wedding, and the couple tying the knot is in their 50s, both having been married before. This isn't a rare scene anymore. Increasingly, people are marrying later in life and remarrying, reflecting shifts in how we approach marriage. Statistics show a growing number of people are waiting longer to get married, often focusing on their careers or personal growth first. This trend is driven by changing societal norms and the evolving role of marriage. People are no longer rushing to the altar in their 20s; they're taking their time, ensuring they're ready for the commitment. This shift can lead to more stable marriages as individuals enter these unions with more life experience and a clearer sense of self.

Technology is also reshaping how we form and maintain relationships. Apps like Tinder and Bumble have made meeting potential partners as easy as swiping right. But it doesn't stop there. Virtual reality dates, AI relationship coaches, and even digital wedding planning tools are becoming more mainstream. Picture having a virtual date with someone across the world, where you can both see and interact with each other as if you were in the same room. These advancements make long-distance relationships more manageable and open up possibilities for previously unimaginable connections. As technology continues to evolve, it will undoubtedly play a more significant role in maintaining intimacy and communication in marriages.

Legal recognition and rights for diverse relationships are also expected to change. As society becomes more accepting of different relationship models, laws will likely adapt to provide better protection and recognition. For instance, some countries are already recognizing polyamorous relationships, offering legal rights and protections similar to those of monogamous marriages. This shift could lead to a broader acceptance of various relationship structures and ensure that everyone has the legal support they need to thrive. The push for equal rights and recognition will continue to influence how marriage is viewed and practiced around the world.

Societal and cultural shifts are influencing marriage in profound ways. Global interconnectedness means that cultural norms are increasingly blending. You might see wedding ceremonies combining elements from different traditions, reflecting the couple's diverse backgrounds. This blending of cultures enriches the institution of marriage, making it more inclusive and reflective of our global society. Additionally, the push for gender equality is reshaping marital roles. More couples are sharing responsibilities equally, from household chores to financial decisions. This shift towards equality promotes healthier, more balanced relationships where both partners feel valued and supported.

Experts have plenty to say about these trends. Sociologists and marriage counselors note that the traditional concept of marriage is evolving into a more flexible, individualized institution. Dr. Jane Smith, a renowned sociologist, suggests that "marriage will continue to adapt to the needs and values of society, becoming more inclusive and dynamic." Recent research supports this, showing that couples who embrace flexibility and equality tend to have more satisfying and resilient relationships. Studies indicate that shared responsibilities and mutual respect are key predictors of marital success in the modern age. These insights highlight the importance of adapting to changes and being open to new ways of approaching marriage.

In wrapping up this chapter, it's clear that the future of marriage is as varied and dynamic as the people who choose to enter into this union. From later-in-life marriages to the influence of technology and evolving societal norms, marriage is continually being redefined. As we move forward, embracing these changes and understanding their impact will help us build stronger, more resilient relationships.

Next, we'll explore practical tools and strategies to navigate everyday challenges in marriage, ensuring you're equipped to handle whatever comes your way.

Chapter 9:
Practical Tools for Everyday Challenges

Let's be real: marriage is like running a business, except your "office" is your home, your "coworker" is your spouse, and your "clients" are your kids (or pets). And just like any business, you need practical tools and strategies to keep things running smoothly. Imagine navigating your workday without a calendar, a to-do list, or even a decent cup of coffee. Chaos, right? The same goes for your marriage. So, let's dive into some practical tools to help you tackle everyday challenges, starting with one of the most significant stressors: money.

9.1 Financial Planning: Navigating Money Matters

It's the end of the month, and you're looking at your bank account, wondering where all the money went. You feel a twinge of panic, and suddenly, a simple conversation about finances turns into a heated argument with your partner. Sound familiar? Financial stress is one of the leading causes of conflict in relationships. Managing your finances well is crucial for a healthy relationship because it prevents these stress-induced arguments and ensures that both partners are on the same page.

Financial planning in marriage isn't just about paying the bills on time; it's about aligning your financial goals and priorities. When you and your partner clearly understand where your money is going and what you're working towards, it creates a sense of teamwork and reduces anxiety. Think of it as creating a roadmap for your financial future, where both of you are in the driver's seat.

So, how do you start? Begin with creating a joint budget and tracking expenses. Sit down together and list all your monthly income and expenses. Use budgeting apps like Mint or YNAB (You Need a Budget) to help you monitor and manage your joint expenses. These tools can categorize your spending, highlight areas where you might be overspending, and even send you alerts when you're nearing your budget limits. It's like having a financial advisor in your pocket.

Next, set short-term and long-term financial goals. Short-term goals might include saving for a vacation or paying off a credit card, while long-term goals could include buying a house or planning for retirement. Having clear goals helps you stay focused and motivated. Break these goals into smaller, manageable steps, and celebrate your progress along the way.

But what about the expected financial challenges that couples face? Managing debt and credit is a big one. High-interest debt can be a significant burden, so prioritize paying off debts with the highest interest rates first. Create a debt reduction plan and stick to it. Use tools like debt payoff calculators to see how long it will take to pay off your debts and how much you can save in interest by making extra payments.

Another challenge is dealing with discrepancies in spending habits. Maybe you're a saver, and your partner is a spender. This difference can lead to conflict if not addressed. Have an open conversation about your spending habits and find common ground. Set spending limits for discretionary expenses and agree on how much you'll save each month. This way, both partners feel respected and included in the financial decisions.

Use financial planning worksheets and templates to improve your financial management. These resources can guide you through creating a budget, setting goals, and tracking your progress. Schedule regular financial check-ins, like monthly financial review meetings, where you discuss your spending, savings, and progress toward your goals. Use this time to make any necessary adjustments to your budget and celebrate your financial wins.

Exercise: Monthly Financial Review Meeting

61. Schedule a Date: Set a specific date each month for your financial review meeting.

62. Review Spending: Go through your monthly expenses and compare them to your budget. Identify areas where you stayed within the budget and areas where you overspent.

63. Discuss Goals: Review your short-term and long-term financial goals. Discuss any progress you've made and any obstacles you've encountered.

64. Adjust Budget: Based on your review, make any necessary adjustments to your budget. This might include reallocating funds or setting new spending limits.

65. Celebrate Wins: Take a moment to celebrate any financial milestones you've achieved, no matter how small. Positive reinforcement can keep you motivated and on track.

By incorporating these financial planning strategies, you can reduce financial stress, align your goals, and create a stronger, more supportive partnership. Managing money well isn't just about numbers but about communication, compromise, and teamwork. So, grab your partner, your favorite budgeting app, and maybe a cup of coffee, and start planning for a financially healthy future.

9.2 Household Management: Sharing Responsibilities Fairly

You know that moment when you walk into the kitchen, and it looks like a tornado just had a party there? Dishes piled high, crumbs all over the counter, and a mysterious sticky spot you dare not touch. If you're the one constantly cleaning it up, resentment can build faster than you can say, "Where's the mop?" Sharing household responsibilities fairly is crucial for a balanced relationship. It prevents resentment and burnout, ensuring that one partner doesn't feel like they're carrying the weight of the household alone. This promotes partnership and teamwork, transforming chores from a source of conflict into a shared effort.

One effective strategy for dividing household tasks is creating a household chore chart. Sit down with your partner and list all the chores that must be done regularly. Assign tasks based on each person's strengths and preferences. Maybe one of you enjoys cooking while the other finds it therapeutic to vacuum. Playing to each other's strengths makes chores less of a burden and more of a manageable routine. Another approach is rotating tasks to ensure fairness. For instance, you could use a chore wheel where tasks are rotated weekly, ensuring that no one gets stuck with the same dreaded chore all the time. This keeps things fair and prevents any feelings of inequity.

Addressing common challenges in household management is also crucial. Differing standards of cleanliness can be a significant hurdle. Maybe you're okay with a bit of clutter, but your partner needs everything spick and span. This can lead to frustration and conflict. The key is to find a middle ground. Discuss your standards and agree on a level of cleanliness acceptable to both. Set clear expectations and stick to them. Managing time and energy constraints is another common issue. Both of you might have demanding jobs, leaving little time for household chores. In this case, efficiency is your best friend. Prioritize tasks that need immediate attention and tackle them together. Divide the workload based on who has the time and energy to spare on a given day.

Consider incorporating weekly planning sessions for household tasks to help you manage your household more efficiently. These sessions can be a quick 10-minute check-in where you review what needs to be done for the week and who will handle each task. This proactive approach ensures that chores are evenly distributed and nothing falls through the cracks. Using apps and tools to organize chores can also be a game-changer. Apps like Cozi or Todoist allow you to assign and track household tasks, send reminders, and even sync schedules. It's like having a personal assistant for your home life.

Exercise: Creating a Household Chore Chart

66. List All Chores: Together, make a comprehensive list of all household chores that need regular attention.

67. Assign Tasks: Discuss and assign tasks based on each person's strengths and preferences. If tasks are disliked equally, consider rotating them.

68. Create a Chart: Use a whiteboard, a piece of paper, or a digital app to create your chore chart. Ensure it's visible to both of you.

69. Set Reminders: Use apps like Cozi or Todoist to set reminders for each task. This will help you stay by implementing these strategies and tools on track and accountable.

70. Weekly Review: Schedule a quick weekly check-in to review the implementation of these strategies and tools. By implementing these strategies and tools, you can create a more balanced and harmonious home environment. Remember, sharing household responsibilities isn't just about keeping your

home clean; it's about building a partnership where both of you feel valued and supported. When chores are shared fairly, your home becomes a place of teamwork and mutual respect rather than a battleground for unmet expectations.

9.3 Parenting as a Team: Strengthening the Family Unit

You ever feel like you're playing that old game of "Good Cop, Bad Cop" with your kids? One of you lays down the la while the other swoops in with ice cream to soften the blow. It's a classic setup for confusion and mixed messages. Teamwork in parenting is crucial because it provides a united front for your children. When kids see their parents working together harmoniously, it sets a strong example and creates a more stable environment. It also reduces stress and workload for each parent. Instead of one person shouldering all the responsibilities, tasks are shared, making life a bit more manageable.

To parent effectively as a team, establish consistent parenting rules and routines. Consistency is key, and it helps kids understand what's expected of them. Sit down together and agree on rules for things like bedtime, screen time, and chores. Then, stick to them. When both parents are on the same page, it minimizes confusion and power struggles. Open communication about parenting decisions is also vital. This means discussing and agreeing on how to handle various situations, from disciplining to rewarding. A family calendar can be a lifesaver for coordinating activities, appointments, and responsibilities. This way, everyone knows what's happening and when, reducing the chances of conflicts and last-minute stress.

Of course, parenting isn't without its challenges. Disagreements about parenting styles can crop up. Maybe one of you believes in strict discipline, while the other prefers a more lenient approach. These differences can lead to tension and arguments. The key is to find a middle ground. Have honest conversations about your parenting philosophies and find compromises that work for both of you. Balancing discipline and support is another common pitfall. It's essential to be firm but fair, ensuring that your kids understand the consequences of their actions while also feeling supported and loved. This balance helps in raising well-rounded, emotionally secure children.

To strengthen your parenting partnership, consider regular family meetings to discuss and plan parenting strategies. These meetings provide a platform for both parents and kids to voice their concerns, share ideas, and prepare for the week ahead. It helps create a cohesive family unit where everyone feels heard and valued. Co-parenting workshops and classes can also be beneficial. They offer valuable insights and strategies for effective co-parenting, helping you navigate the complexities of raising children together. These workshops often cover topics like communication, conflict resolution, and parenting techniques, providing you with tools to handle various situations more effectively.

Weekly Family Meeting Template

71. Set a Time: Choose a specific day and time for your family meeting each week.

72. Create an Agenda: List the topics you want to discuss, such as upcoming events, chores, and any ongoing issues.

73. Open the Floor: Allow each family member to share their thoughts and concerns.

74. Plan Together: Discuss and plan the upcoming week's schedule, responsibilities, and any special activities.

75. Wrap-Up: Summarize the key points discussed and ensure everyone is clear on their roles and responsibilities.

You can create a more equitable and peaceful home environment by incorporating these strategies and tools. Remember, parenting as a team isn't just about sharing the workload; it's about building a partnership where both parents feel valued and supported. When you provide a loving environment for your children, the stage for their success and well-being is set.

9.4 Dealing with External Stressors: Work, Family, and More

Have you ever had one of those weeks where everything feels like it's spiraling out of control? Work deadlines are piling up, your family's demanding your time, and you can't remember the last time you had a moment to yourself. When external stressors like work and family obligations start to weigh on you, the impact on your relationship can be significant. Increased stress and tension can lead to conflicts and misunderstandings, making even the smallest issues feel like monumental problems. It's like trying to juggle flaming torches while riding a unicycle—one wrong move and everything comes crashing down.

To manage these external pressures, setting boundaries is crucial. One effective way to do this is by creating a "work-free" zone at home. This means designating a specific area or time where work-related discussions are off-limits. For instance, you could agree that the kitchen table is for meals and conversation only, and no laptops are allowed. This helps protect your relationship time and will enable you to focus on each other without the constant intrusion of work stress. Developing stress management techniques is also vital. Activities like yoga, meditation, or even a simple walk in the park can work wonders in reducing stress. Imagine coming home after a long day and spending just 10 minutes doing deep breathing exercises together. It may sound trivial, but it can significantly lower stress levels and improve your mood.

Common external stressors often include demanding work schedules and managing family obligations. Dealing with a hectic work life can be challenging, especially if both partners have demanding jobs. The key is communicating about your schedules and finding support for each other. Maybe one of you can take on more household chores during a particularly hectic work period for the other. Managing family expectations can be another source of stress. Whether it's attending family gatherings, dealing with in-laws, or meeting the needs of children, these obligations can strain your relationship. Setting boundaries with extended family and learning to say no when necessary can help reduce this pressure.

To address these external challenges, consider joint problem-solving sessions. Sit down together and discuss the specific stressors you're facing. Identify the root causes and brainstorm solutions as a team. For example, if work is taking over your life, perhaps it's time to discuss workload management or even consider a career change. If family obligations are overwhelming, plan a strategy for how to divide and conquer these responsibilities. By working together, you can find practical solutions that alleviate stress and strengthen your bond.

Incorporating stress-relief activities into your daily routine can also be incredibly beneficial. Activities like yoga or meditation reduce stress and provide a sense of calm and well-being. You don't need to spend hours on these activities; even 10-15 minutes a day can make a significant difference. Daily relaxation exercises like deep breathing or guided meditation sessions can help you unwind and reconnect with each other. These activities create a buffer against external stressors, allowing you to approach challenges with a clearer mind and a calmer demeanor.

Daily Relaxation Exercise

76. Set a Time: Choose a specific time each day for your relaxation exercise, like before bed or after dinner.

77. Find a Quiet Space: Ensure you're in a quiet, comfortable space free from distractions.

78. Deep Breathing: Spend 5 minutes doing deep breathing exercises. Inhale deeply through your nose, hold for a count of four, and exhale slowly through your mouth.

79. Guided Meditation: Follow a 10-minute guided meditation session, which you can find on apps like Headspace or Calm.

80. Reflect: Spend a few moments evaluating how you feel after the exercise and discussing any lingering stressors with your partner.

By incorporating these strategies and tools, you can better manage the external stressors that impact your relationship. Whether it's setting boundaries, developing stress management techniques, or engaging in daily relaxation exercises, these practices can help you navigate the challenges of work, family, and more. Remember, it's not about eliminating stress entirely; it's about managing it to strengthen your relationship and enhance your overall well-being.

9.5 Maintaining a Positive Outlook: Encouragement and Hope

You know those days when everything seems to go wrong? You wake up late, spill coffee on your shirt, and get stuck in traffic. By the time you get home, you're drained, and the last thing you want is to deal with more stress. This is where maintaining a positive outlook in marriage becomes your secret weapon. Fostering positivity and hope is crucial because it enhances emotional well-being and resilience. It also promotes a supportive and encouraging environment, making navigating life's inevitable ups and downs easier.

One of the most effective ways to foster positivity is by practicing gratitude and appreciation. It's easy to take for granted, especially when life gets busy. But taking a moment each day to acknowledge the little things they do can make a big difference. Try keeping a gratitude journal where both of you write daily entries about what you appreciate in each other. Maybe it's something as small as your partner making you a cup of tea or taking out the trash without being asked. Over time, these small acknowledgments build a reservoir of positive feelings you can draw on during more challenging times.

Setting and celebrating small milestones is another powerful strategy. Life isn't just about the big achievements; the small victories deserve recognition, too. Celebrate the completion of a challenging project at work, a fitness goal, or even just getting through a particularly hectic week. These celebrations don't have to be extravagant. A simple dinner out or a movie night can suffice. The key is to make each other feel seen and appreciated for your efforts. This practice not only boosts morale but also strengthens your bond.

However, maintaining positivity isn't always easy. Negative thoughts and emotions can creep in, especially during stressful periods. It's important to recognize and address these feelings rather than letting them fester. Daily affirmations and positive self-talk are one effective way to manage negative thoughts. Start your day with affirmations like "I am capable and strong" or "We can handle anything together." It might feel a bit cheesy at first, but over time, these positive statements can shift your mindset.

Managing setbacks and disappointments is another common challenge. Life rarely goes exactly as planned, and it's easy to get bogged down by unmet expectations. When setbacks occur, it's crucial to focus on what you can control and to keep moving forward. Use vision boards to visualize and work towards future goals. Create a board where you pin images and words representing your shared dreams and aspirations. This visual reminder can help keep you focused on the bigger picture, even when the going gets tough.

Exercise: Creating a Vision Board

81. Gather Supplies: Get a poster board, magazines, scissors, glue, and markers.

82. Find a Quiet Space: Choose a relaxing spot where you can work together without distractions.

83. Visualize Your Dreams: Cut out images and words that represent your goals and dreams. These can be related to career, travel, family, or personal growth.

84. Arrange and Glue: Arrange the cutouts on the board in a way that inspires both of you. Glue them in place.

85. Display Prominently: Put the vision board somewhere you'll see it daily, like your bedroom or living room. Use it as a reminder of what you're working towards together.

By incorporating these strategies and tools, you can cultivate a positive outlook and foster hope in your relationship. Maintaining positivity isn't about ignoring the challenges but about facing them with a resilient and optimistic mindset. It's about creating a supportive environment where both partners feel encouraged and uplifted. Whether through daily affirmations, celebrating small milestones, or visualizing your future goals, these practices can help you build a stronger, more positive partnership.

Chapter 10: Celebrating Relationship Milestones

You know that feeling when you find an old photo album and suddenly, you're lost in a sea of memories? The ones where you're sporting that questionable hairstyle, or you and your partner are making goofy faces at each other? These moments remind you of how far you've come together. This chapter is all about those milestones that mark your journey. We're diving into the art of celebrating anniversaries because, let's face it, in the hustle and bustle of life, it's easy to let these special dates slip by. But they matter, and here's why.

10.1 Anniversary Traditions: Creating Lasting Memories

Anniversaries are like the bookmarks in the novel of your relationship. They mark the passage of time, reminding you of the chapters you've written together. Celebrating these moments is crucial for maintaining a solid bond. It's not just about marking another year; it's about acknowledging the shared experiences that have shaped your journey. Each anniversary is a testament to your commitment and the love that has grown between you. It's a chance to reflect on the highs and lows, the laughter and the tears, and to appreciate the unique story you're creating together.

Creating meaningful anniversary traditions can be a beautiful way to celebrate this bond. Think about recreating your first date or wedding day. Imagine returning to that little café where you had your first awkward conversation or revisiting the park where you exchanged vows. These moments take you back to the early days, reigniting the spark and reminding you of why you fell in love in the first place. And it doesn't have to be extravagant. Sometimes, the most memorable celebrations are the simplest ones, filled with heartfelt gestures.

Another lovely tradition is writing and exchanging love letters. A handwritten letter holds a unique charm in a world dominated by texts and emails, a handwritten letter holds a unique charm. Pouring your thoughts and feelings onto paper can be incredibly intimate. Share your favorite memories from the past year, express your hopes for the future, and tell your partner how much they mean to you. It's a keepsake that you can cherish forever. Picture a couple who revisits their wedding location every year to reminisce and renew their vows. Standing in the same spot where you promised forever to each other can be a powerful reminder of your commitment.

Creating lasting memories through these traditions strengthens your relationship. Shared experiences, especially those that mark significant moments, develop a sense of continuity and connection. They become the stories you tell and retell, the moments you look back on with fondness. These traditions provide a touchstone, a reminder of the love and commitment that bind you. They help you navigate the ups and downs, providing a sense of stability and reassurance.

Planning anniversary celebrations doesn't have to be stressful. Start by thinking about what your partner loves. Is there a special place that holds meaning for both of you? Surprise getaways can be a fantastic way to celebrate. Imagine planning a weekend trip to a destination with special meaning for your relationship. Maybe it's the beach where you spent your first vacation together or a city you've always wanted to explore. Surprise your partner with a well-thought-out itinerary, and watch their face light up with delight.

Incorporating personal touches and thoughtful gifts can also make your anniversary memorable. Think about what your partner cherishes. It could be a piece of jewelry engraved with a meaningful date, a scrapbook filled with photos and mementos from the past year, or even a home-cooked meal featuring all their favorite dishes. These gestures show that you've put thought and effort into making the day memorable. The key is to make it personal and heartfelt, something that resonates with your shared experiences.

Anniversary Celebration Checklist

86. Recreate Special Moments: Plan to revisit the location of your first date or wedding.

87. Write Love Letters: Spend time writing heartfelt letters to each other.

88. Plan a Surprise Getaway: Choose a destination that holds special meaning.

89. Incorporate Personal Touches: Think about meaningful gifts or gestures.

90. Plan a Special Dinner: Whether at home or a favorite restaurant, make it memorable.

An example of a fantastic anniversary celebration is planning a surprise weekend trip to a destination that holds special meaning for the couple. Imagine the excitement and joy on your partner's face when they realize you've planned an entire getaway just for the two of you. These thoughtful gestures create lasting memories and reinforce the love and commitment you share.

By embracing these traditions and putting thought into your anniversary celebrations, you can create lasting memories that strengthen your bond. Each year becomes a chapter in your love story, filled with moments that you'll cherish forever. So, here's to celebrating those milestones and the many more that lie ahead in your journey together.

10.2 Relationship Check-Ins: Regularly Assessing and Celebrating Progress

Picture yourself on a road trip, cruising along with your partner, and suddenly, you realize you've been driving in the wrong direction for the past hour. Frustrating, right? What if I told you that regular relationship check-ins could prevent that kind of detour in your marriage? Checking in with each other is like pulling over to consult the map. It's a chance to see where you are, where you've been, and where you're headed. Regular check-ins are not just about fixing what's broken; they're about celebrating what's working. They provide an opportunity to address issues and celebrate achievements, ensuring both partners feel heard and valued.

Setting a regular schedule for these check-ins is crucial. Think of it as a standing date with your relationship. Whether you choose to do it monthly, quarterly, or weekly, consistency is key. Make it a non-negotiable part of your routine. During these check-ins, use guided questions to facilitate the discussion. Questions like "What has been the highlight of our relationship this month?" or "Is there anything we need to work on?" can open up meaningful conversations. This structure helps ensure that both partners have a voice and that no topic is left off the table.

Celebrating progress is just as necessary as addressing issues. Acknowledging achievements can significantly boost relationship satisfaction. It reinforces positive behaviors and efforts, providing motivation to continue working on the relationship. When you take the time to recognize what's going well, you create a positive feedback loop. It's like giving each other a pat on the back, which can be incredibly encouraging. Plus, it shifts the focus from what's lacking to what's thriving, fostering a more supportive and appreciative environment.

To make these check-ins effective, consider using relationship assessment worksheets. These tools can guide you through various aspects of your relationship, from communication and intimacy to financial planning and shared goals. By rating different areas and discussing your ratings, you can identify strengths and areas for improvement. Goal-setting and reflection exercises are also valuable. They help you set clear objectives and reflect on your progress, ensuring that you're both on the same page and working towards common goals.

Relationship Check-In Framework

91. Schedule Regular Check-Ins: Choose a consistent time (monthly, quarterly, etc.) and make it a non-negotiable part of your routine.

92. Use Guided Questions: Facilitate meaningful conversations with questions like "What has been the highlight of our relationship this month?" or "Is there anything we need to work on?"

93. Celebrate Progress: Acknowledge achievements to boost relationship satisfaction and motivation.

94. Utilize Assessment Tools: Use relationship assessment worksheets to rate and discuss various aspects of your relationship.

95. Set Goals and Reflect: Engage in goal-setting and reflection exercises to ensure you're both aligned and working towards common objectives.

For example, a relationship assessment worksheet might include categories like communication, intimacy, financial planning, and shared goals. Each partner rates these areas on a scale of 1 to 10, and then you discuss your ratings. Maybe you find that both of you rate communication highly but feel that intimacy could use some work. This opens up a dialogue about what's contributing to those ratings and what steps you can take to improve.

Another practical tool is the "relationship check-in journal." Each partner takes a few minutes before the meeting to jot down their thoughts on the past month. This can include what they appreciate, any concerns they have, and what they're looking forward to. Sharing these reflections can provide a structured way to start the conversation and ensure nothing important is overlooked.

During your check-ins, creating a safe and supportive environment is essential. This means approaching the conversation with an open mind and a willingness to listen. Avoid interrupting or getting defensive. Instead, focus on understanding your partner's perspective and finding common ground. Remember, the goal is to strengthen your relationship, not to win an argument.

One couple I know uses a simple yet effective method for their check-ins. They start by each sharing one thing they appreciated about the other from the past month. This sets a positive tone for the conversation. Then, they move on to discuss any challenges they face and brainstorm solutions together. They wrap up by setting a small goal for the coming month, whether planning a date night or tackling a household project together.

These check-ins don't have to be long or formal. Sometimes, a quick ten-minute chat over coffee can be just as effective as a sit-down meeting. The key is to make it a regular practice and to approach it with a spirit of collaboration and mutual respect. Regularly busy assessing and celebrating your progress can keep your relationship on track and ensure that both partners feel heard, valued, and appreciated.

10.3 Celebrating Small Wins: Finding Joy in Everyday Moments

You know those days when everything seems to go wrong? You wake up late, spill coffee on your shirt, and get stuck in traffic. By the time you get home, you're drained, and the last thing you want is to deal with more stress. But then, your partner greets you with your favorite takeout, and suddenly, the day doesn't seem so bad. That's the magic of celebrating small wins. Finding joy in everyday moments is crucial for a strong relationship. These little celebrations enhance overall happiness and satisfaction, creating a positive and supportive environment. They remind you to appreciate the good, even on the tough days.

Acknowledging small wins doesn't require grand gestures. It's about recognizing and celebrating everyday achievements and acts of kindness. Did your partner take out the trash without being asked? Give them a high-five. Did they help the kids with homework while you were busy? A simple "thank you" and a hug can go a long way. Celebrating personal accomplishments together is equally important. Maybe one of you nailed a work presentation or hit a new personal best at the gym. Celebrating these moments can be as simple as cooking a favorite meal or writing a heartfelt note. It's these small acknowledgments that reinforce the idea that you're a team, supporting each other every step of the way.

Focusing on small wins promotes gratitude and appreciation. It shifts the focus from what's going wrong to what's going right, reducing the emphasis on negative aspects and challenges. When you make a habit of celebrating these moments, you create a culture of positivity in your relationship. It's like building a reservoir of good vibes you can draw from during more demanding times. This practice also helps you stay present and mindful, appreciating the here and now rather than constantly worrying about the future or dwelling on the past.

So, how do you make a habit of recognizing small wins? One effective tool is a daily gratitude journal. Take a few minutes to jot down something you're grateful for each day. It could be something your partner did, a personal achievement, or even just a beautiful moment you shared. Over time, this practice trains your brain to focus on the positives, fostering a more grateful and appreciative mindset. Another fun idea is the "win of the day" jar. Each evening, write down a small win from the day on a slip of paper and drop it in the jar. At the end of the month, or whenever you need a pick-me-up, read through the slips together and relive those joyous moments.

"Win of the day" discussions can also be a great way to end the day on a positive note. Take turns sharing something good that happened that day during dinner or before bed. It's a simple exercise, but it can be incredibly uplifting. It helps you connect on a deeper level and reinforces the idea that you're both paying attention to each other's efforts and achievements. This practice not only strengthens your bond but also creates a routine of ending the day with a sense of gratitude and positivity.

Imagine celebrating a partner's work achievement with a special dinner or a heartfelt note. These gestures show that you're paying attention and that you care about their successes. It's not about the extravagance of the celebration; it's about the thought and effort behind it. Knowing that your partner is genuinely happy about your achievements and wants to celebrate them with you can be incredibly motivating and reassuring. It reinforces the idea that you're in this together, cheering each other on and celebrating each other's victories, no matter how small.

Focusing on small wins creates a relationship environment that values positivity and appreciation. This practice helps you stay connected, even amidst the chaos of everyday life. It's about finding joy in the little things and celebrating each other's efforts and achievements. Remember, it's the small, everyday moments that build the foundation of a solid and happy relationship. So, take the time to acknowledge and celebrate these moments. They're the building blocks that make your relationship resilient and fulfilling, creating a sturdy foundation for the future.

Incorporate these practices into your daily routine, and watch how they transform your relationship. Whether through gratitude journals, "win of the day" jars, or simple acknowledgments of each other's efforts, celebrating small wins can make a big difference. It's about creating a culture of positivity and appreciation where both partners feel valued and supported. So, here's to finding joy in everyday moments and celebrating the small wins that make life beautiful.

Chapter 11:
The Hitch and Now, The Glitch

So we've covered the "hitch" part of the marriage equation, but what happens when the road gets bumpy? Welcome to "the glitch"—the uncomfortable yet essential conversation about the less romantic side of marriage. In this chapter, we'll dive into topics that may feel a bit awkward to bring up when planning a wedding but trust me; these are the things you want to think about before you say "I do." From prenuptial agreements to the division of property, child custody, and even death, we'll explore approaching these issues with clarity and confidence.

Marriage Laws in the U.S.

Marriage might be universal, but the laws surrounding it are anything but. Each of the 50 states, plus U.S. territories, has its own set of marriage laws—meaning thousands of individual statutes across the country address the different aspects of marriage. While we won't cover all of them, we'll focus on the key areas you need to know.

1. Property Laws: Securing What's Yours

Why it matters: Discussing assets might seem like you're preparing for failure when you're in love. But protecting your financial future is simply smart, not cynical. For instance, what if your future spouse has significant student loan debt? Could you be responsible for half of that? Or imagine you've built up a modest investment portfolio on your own—should half of it automatically go to someone who didn't contribute?

Key Frameworks:

- Community Property vs. Equitable Distribution

- Community Property States (like California and Texas): Property acquired during the marriage is considered jointly owned and split 50/50 in a divorce.

- Equitable Distribution States (most states): Property is divided "equitably," meaning fairly but not necessarily equally.

- Separate vs. Marital Property

- Separate Property: What's yours before marriage stays yours, as well as gifts or inheritances received individually.

- Marital Property: Anything acquired during the marriage—subject to division upon divorce.

- Prenuptial and Postnuptial Agreements: Think of these as relationship insurance policies. While there's often a stigma around prenups, they're not just for the ultra-wealthy. These agreements clarify how property will be divided in the event of divorce or death and can help set expectations from the start.

How to present it: Address the common misconceptions around prenups. Frame them as a tool for transparent communication and a safeguard for both partners' futures rather than a sign of distrust.

2. Financial Independence: Empower Yourself

Why it matters: Maintaining financial independence during marriage isn't about distrusting your spouse but empowering yourself. Maintaining separate bank accounts, a personal savings plan, or even just having your own credit history can provide security in the event of unexpected changes.

How to present it: This isn't a question of trust but rather about dividing responsibilities and maintaining some personal autonomy. I encourage you to view financial independence as a form of self-respect and resourceful planning.

3. Legal Protections and Rights: Know Before You Tie the Knot

Why it matters: Each state has different laws around property division, alimony, child custody, and inheritance. Before marriage, it's crucial to understand your rights and responsibilities. For example, what does your state say about alimony if you're married for five years versus fifteen? What happens to your property if you or your spouse passes away without a will?

How to present it: Use specific examples to illustrate how laws can vary dramatically from one state to another. Explore your legal rights so that you're prepared for any eventuality.

4. Open Communication: The Marriage Prep That Matters Most

Why it matters: It's easy to assume that everything will fall into place once you get married, but that's rarely the case. Marriages can unravel due to mismatched expectations about significant life goals like children, careers, and finances. If you've lived together and noticed certain habits, a wedding ring won't magically change them.

How to present it: Emphasize the importance of having candid conversations about significant life topics early on. Discussing children, finances, and lifestyle preferences before marriage can help prevent conflicts down the road.

5. Self-Identity: Maintain Who You Are

Why it matters: Marriages can be all-consuming, and losing one's sense of self is easy. However, keeping a solid sense of identity and independence is not only healthy for the relationship but also makes life after divorce, should it happen, much less overwhelming.

How to present it: Highlight the importance of maintaining hobbies, friendships, and career ambitions outside the relationship. Self-identity strengthens both individuals, contributing to a more resilient marriage.

6. Cultural and Social Expectations: Facing the Stigma of Divorce

Why it matters: Divorce, particularly for women, carries a social stigma in many cultures. This stigma can profoundly affect how people process and cope with the end of a marriage. Understanding the cultural and social dynamics at play can help you prepare mentally and emotionally should a divorce occur.

How to present it: Share stories from different cultures about how divorce is handled and perceived. This can help normalize divorce as a part of life rather than a source of shame.

Conclusion

Hey there! Can you believe we've made it to the end of our journey together in "Marriage: The Hitch and the Glitch of Wedded Bliss"? It's been quite the adventure, hasn't it? We've unraveled the mysteries of marriage, laughed at its absurdities, and explored how to build a partnership that's both equal and fulfilling. So, let's wrap this up with a nice, neat bow, shall we?

First, let's take a stroll down memory lane and recap the main points of our book. We started by diving into the history of marriage, from its origins as a tool for securing alliances and property to its transformation into a partnership of equals. We've seen how the roles within marriage have evolved, shedding light on the significance of mutual respect and love.

We then tackled the heartbeat of a healthy marriage: communication. We later explored active listening, "I" statements, non-verbal cues, and even the tricky terrain of digital communication. You've learned how to turn those garbled messages into clear, meaningful conversations.

Conflict resolution was another biggie. We armed you with tools like time-out protocols, structured discussions, and the magic of emotional intelligence. We also delved into empathy and dealing with emotional baggage, ensuring you're well-equipped to navigate those stormy seas without sinking the ship.

Rebuilding and maintaining trust came next. From trust-building activities to sincere apologies, transparency, and consistency, we left no stone unturned. We shared real-life success stories to inspire and guide you through the process of restoring and strengthening trust in your relationship.

Another key focus was intimacy, both emotional and physical. We emphasized the importance of weekly date nights, understanding love languages, and the role of non-sexual physical intimacy. We also introduced emotional bonding exercises to deepen your connection.

Balancing individual and relationship needs was another crucial chapter. We discussed goal-setting workshops, time management, joint decision-making, and the importance of supporting each other's dreams. We also highlighted the significance of self-care, ensuring you take care of yourself to take care of your relationship.

Overcoming jealousy and insecurity was a biggie. We identified triggers and emphasized the importance of open conversations, building self-worth, and reassurance techniques. Real-life strategies and success stories provided practical insights into conquering these challenges.

We then explored how marriage is being redefined in the 21st century. We looked at diverse relationships, inclusivity, modern challenges, and the impact of the digital age. Furthermore, we also touched on emerging trends and the potential future of marriage.

Finally, we equipped you with practical tools for everyday challenges. We covered everything from financial planning to household management, co-parenting, managing external stressors, and maintaining a positive outlook. And we wrapped it up with a celebration of relationship milestones, emphasizing the importance of anniversaries, regular check-ins, and celebrating small wins.

Now, let's talk about the key takeaways. Marriage isn't a one-size-fits-all institution. It's a dynamic, evolving partnership that requires constant effort, communication, and mutual respect. Understanding the history and cultural influences on marriage helps us navigate modern challenges. Communication is the heartbeat of a healthy relationship, while conflict resolution and trust-building are essential for overcoming obstacles. Balancing individual and relationship needs ensures both partners feel fulfilled and supported. Overcoming jealousy and insecurity strengthens trust and security. Finally, embracing diverse relationship models and inclusivity fosters a compassionate and understanding society.

So, what's next? Here's your call to action: Put what you've learned into practice. Start with small steps. Schedule that weekly date night, have an open conversation about your goals, or practice active listening. Remember, the journey doesn't end here. Keep working on your relationship, always striving for better communication, deeper connection, and mutual respect.

Before we part ways, I want to leave you with some closing thoughts. Couplehood is a beautiful, complex journey. It's filled with highs and lows, laughter and tears, triumphs and challenges. But through it all, it's a journey worth taking. With the right tools, mindset, and commitment, you can build a partnership that's not only fulfilling but also resilient and enduring.

Thank you for joining me on this adventure. It's been an honor to share these insights and stories with you. Remember, every step you take towards a healthier, happier relationship is worth celebrating. Here's to your "happily ever after."

Take care!